Quid Pro Quo

Quid Pro Quo

This For That

John S. Burgess
Edited by Amy E Ambry

88249 — May 2005

Writer's Showcase
San Jose New York Lincoln Shanghai

Quid Pro Quo
This For That

All Rights Reserved © 2001 by John S. Burgess

Writer's Showcase
an imprint of iUniverse.com, Inc.

For information address:
iUniverse.com, Inc.
5220 S 16th, Ste. 200
Lincoln, NE 68512
www.iuniverse.com

ISBN: 0-595-19991-7
3 5944 00088 2496
Printed in the United States of America

CHAPTER 1

This could not be.

This could not be the St. Charles Avenue apartment where twelve hours earlier four young couples came together to celebrate their graduation from the highly regarded Tulane University Law School.

Blood was everywhere. Splashed across the kitchen counter and up the walls. Droplets fell from the ceiling leaving behind tiny brown stalactites drying on the white plaster. Rust red rivers ran from the sticky pond in the middle of the kitchen floor to a low point in the corner of the room. Tables and chairs were smashed and overturned. Wine bottles and beer cans littered the living room, and the heat of another Fat City summer was beginning to fill the air with the putrid smell of death.

In the middle of this bloody mess lay the twisted and slashed body of a once beautiful 25 year-old women. Mary Ellen Simmons, Summa Cum Laude, Law Review, popular. So promising was her career that she had already accepted a position prior to graduation with a prestigious Washington law firm. It was the best of many offers she had considered. The little black party dress that had complemented her so much the night before was pulled up revealing deep slashes across her thighs. A broken string of pearls, a graduation present from him, lay embedded in the congealing blood under her head and long blond hair.

He was John Stevens, her classmate, and since third year, someone who had been very special in her life. They had fallen very much in love during the last several months and both were so caught up in the joys and promises of their young lives that neither could have imagined the terrible fate that would so completely destroy their lives in such short a time.

Last night he and Mary along with six friends enjoyed an exquisite meal at Café Giovanni on Decatur Street in the French Quarter. Chef Duke LaCiscero added his personal touch to make the meal extra special. The wine flowed freely and spirits were high. With Tulane Law School behind them, John and Mary and four of the others had great cause to celebrate. The remaining two friends were undergraduates. They had all worked very hard, and this was their last night to celebrate before going home.

After dinner they walked up Decatur Street and crossed over to Royal. The four girls paused to look into the expensive shop windows as they strolled along Royal Street. Another left turn, and they passed by the famous Pat O'Brien's. A few doors down, authentic New Orleans jazz poured out of Preservation Hall, played, as it had been for decades, by old timers sitting on wooden crates. The graduates were unconsciously being drawn like lemmings to the infamous Bourbon Street.

Turning left on Bourbon they started back toward Canal Street, laughing at the repulsive sites and smells that had so captivated them as naive first year students. Stale beer, piles of horse shit, vomit, leather clad gays outrageously acting out, gutter punks eating out of overflowing garbage cans, blaring music, strip joints, and, as always, in the middle of all this insanity, there were the seven and eight year old black kids tap dancing for nickels and dimes. This was Bourbon Street, where millions of people came year after year to have fun.

The guys bought **Giant Ass Beers** as advertised at a sidewalk bar, and they all paused briefly outside of the Jazz Café to listen to some amazing lead guitar work. Proceeding down Bourbon Street, and across Canal to St. Charles, they caught the streetcar back to John Steven's apartment.

The celebration continued into the night. They laughed about Bourbon Street. They danced. They joked. They drank and they argued. Sometime after two in the morning, while relieving himself, Stevens lost his balance and fell backwards into the bathtub, so drunk that he didn't feel his head hit the porcelain soap dish.

There he remained until ten o'clock the next morning, when he awoke with the worst headache he had ever known. A gash on the side of his head trickled blood, and his body was so contorted with pain that he doubted his ability to ever straighten out his six-foot frame again. Easing himself carefully out of the tub, he grabbed for the toilet, but the lid was down and he vomited Veal Piccata all over the bathroom.

The pride that the budding young barrister had felt the night before was gone. In its place now was shame and disgust that made his pain even more unbearable. Convinced that this was the worst experience of his life, Stevens had no idea of the horror that awaited him on the other side of the bathroom door.

That was two hours ago. Before the police arrived. Before the house was wrapped in yellow crime scene tape. Before the crowd had gathered outside, and before he was read the Miranda Rights.

As he sat on a kitchen chair, head in hands, his hangover clouded the stark reality of the situation. The apartment was filled with police - some in uniform - others in shirts and ties. There was a photographer snapping pictures. The young man could hear the voices but he did not seem to understand the words.

"Mr. Stevens we gonna be taken y'all downtown shortly, and ya can call whoever y'all like from there, but I wonder if y'all wouldn't mind going over this thing one more time." Sergeant Bell was black, over six feet tall and weighed about two hundred and eighty pounds. As he turned toward Stevens, he seemed to be moving and talking in slow motion. Stevens leaned forward trying to understand, but he could not take his eyes off the body of Mary, now covered with a bed sheet. "Mr. Stevens, did y'all hear me? Are you alright?"

"Ah, yes. I think so." He was jolted by Bell's booming voice.

This **thing** that Sergeant Bell wanted to know about just couldn't be happening. Not to him, and not to Mary - his Mary, so young and so beautiful. "Sergeant, I told you everything I can remember. I don't know what happened here. Mary was fine. We were having a party. I passed out, and that's all I can remember."

"Were there other people with you last night?" Bell asked.

"Yes, there were other people. Of course. I told you that. We all had dinner and came back here to party." Stevens ran his fingers through his hair trying desperately to recall the events of last night.

"Some party." Bell mumbled under his breath.

"Look, we were with Churchill, Feeny, his girlfriend Karen, Patrick Healy, Allison McKay and, Courtney Roberts. You need to talk to them. I need to talk to them. What the hell happened here? I need to know what happened."

"Yeah, well we gonna talk to all them folks soon enough. Right now we gonna put y'all in a patrol car and take y'all downtown where we can help y'all sort this thing out." Bell reached under his arm and helped him to his feet.

CHAPTER 2

The graduation ceremony had been wonderful. It was an all day affair with the Law School Commencement scheduled later in the afternoon. Tom Stevens and his wife Katherine could not have been more proud of their son. At 25, John was their baby - the youngest of four. They loved all their kids and worked hard together for thirty-six years to give them every opportunity they could afford. The years that Tom spent on the road selling medical supplies provided a good home and a happy life for the family, but certainly nothing extravagant. At six foot tall and two hundred and ten pounds, he was a strong but gentle man. He was proud of all his kids, but today it was John who made him stand even taller. He and Katherine had instilled in their kids the same values they had learned from their own parents; honesty, hard work, perseverance, and respect for others. It had not been easy, but the occasional very special days like this made it all worthwhile.

Tom and Katherine taught by example. They were both fifty-eight and practiced what they preached. Through the years they had made many solid friendships, on the job, in the schools, and within the community. The entire Stevens Family had come to be respected and admired in the little historic town of Bay St. Louis, Mississippi, where they had lived for twenty-two years.

The three older Steven's kids had left the nest by the time John was a senior at Tulane. The older sons Matthew and Michael were married. Matt, handsome and well built, was an advertising executive living in Houston, and Michael had recently moved to Chicago with his wife to take a job with her father's brokerage firm. Michael was little over weight, and lacked the confidence of his older brother. Martha, the daughter between Matt and Mike, was diminutive and energetic. She had set out for Washington, D.C. a year earlier with a new Masters Degree in Political Science and high hopes of joining a congressional staff. She had not achieved that goal as yet, but she had landed a good job, and made some friends. She loved the Washington scene.

All three had arrived in New Orleans to join their folks and the guest of honor for dinner on Saturday evening. Matt's wife and Mike's both joined the reunion. It had been a wonderful evening, starting at Mr. B's, one of the Brennan family's best know restaurants. They ate gumbo, and oysters, red snapper, and tender filet. Katherine, who loved to eat, could not resist the roasted veal chop, covered in a rich crabmeat cream sauce. They finished with the house specialty, white chocolate bread pudding in raison rum sauce. After finishing a final cup of New Orleans's famous coffee, the family returned to the Montelione Hotel to continue reminiscing and telling family stories.

The following morning, Graduation Day, they met for breakfast and then walked over to St. Louis Cathedral to attend Mass. It was a beautiful Sunday morning, and the historic gothic cathedral looking out on Jackson Square seemed a fitting place for Tom and Katherine Stevens to give thanks for this wonderful family that had come together to celebrate the accomplishment of its youngest member. After Mass it was back to the hotel to pack and checkout. Then they were all off to the Super Dome for the main event.

The Dome was awesome, like some massive alien space ship that landed the middle of downtown New Orleans, dwarfing everything around it. The University had leased the structure for the commencement exercises, and had lavishly decorated an enormous center stage with stately marble Romanesque columns, multicolored flags, and blankets of beautiful flowers. With the lights turned down, a spotlight featured an impressive gold embossed Tulane University Seal, which seemed to float above the speaker's podium. A green glamae curtain extended the full length of the stage forming a pleated backdrop that sparkled with the reflection of hundreds of flashing cameras. Elevated rows of dignitaries, in their finest, multi-colored, ceremonial caps and gowns, filled the stage. Golden hash marks, stitched on their sleeves, distinguished their rank in the Army of Academia.

Amazed by the splendor of it all, the Stevens Family found seven seats in the mezzanine, high enough to see the gallery of graduates and the entire stage. This was the fifth commencement ceremony for their family, but it was special. Tom and Katherine spotted their son bobbing in the ocean of black caps and gowns, and could not take their eyes off him. Even as speaker after speaker droned on about the great challenges and opportunities that lay ahead they could not contain their excitement.

Finally, with the pontificating done, the long awaited procession began. One by one the new Doctors of Juris Prudence approached the stage to accept their diplomas and shake the hands of the professors who had changed their lives. The P's, the Q's, the R's, and finally the S's. There were just 14 names between Saari and Stevens, and Tom held his breath as his son approached the stage.

"**John Andrew Stevens**" The name echoed through the cavernous Super Dome. Tom allowed himself to exhale, as his son reached for his diploma and accepted the congratulations of Dean Sherman.

"My God." He said, so that only he could hear. "He made it."

As the young man exited stage left, Tom and Katherine looked at each other, and smiled. No words were necessary. Their joy, their pride, and their love was in their eyes.

When Arthur Zolenda stepped off the stage, the Super Dome exploded. Thousands of colored balloons dropped from the steel ribs supporting the great dome, as the graduates and families let out a roar like Mike Ditka and the Saints could only dream about.

After the ceremony, there were pictures to be taken, a lot of hugging to do, and some sad goodbyes as the graduates exchanged e-mail addresses and promised to stay in touch.

Matt, Mike, and Martha had scheduled flights out of New Orleans for early that evening so they could be back at work on Monday morning. They said their goodbyes to John, and the three brothers exchanged awkward hugs. Martha held on to John a little longer, making him promise to visit her in Washington.

"Mom and Dad, it was a wonderful weekend." Martha tried not to cry.

"Great, Dad." Mike rescued Martha, choking back his own emotions. "Mom, we love you."

Matt, the oldest brother, tried to lighten the mood. "Counselor, you take care of the folks, now." He said, turning toward John. "Keep them out of trouble." He put his arms around both his parents. "What can I say, Mom, Dad? Thanks for everything. It was great." He gave them both a hug. "Take care of yourselves, and we will see you again at Christmas."

"Yes. We can't wait." Katherine did not want to show the sadness she felt every time the family parted. "Hope you all can make it. I'll fry the biggest turkey I can find."

Sensing his family was tired and on an emotional over load, Tom took control and hailed a cab, while removing the suitcases from the trunk of his car. With the luggage loaded into the cab, there was nothing left to say or do. Tom, Katherine and John waved as the yellow Royal Taxi pulled away and disappeared up Poydras Street.

The spotlight again quickly refocused on John. Katherine was disappointed when he informed his parents the night before that he was planning to have dinner with some special friends after graduation, and would not be going home with them. But she understood, and felt better when he promised to be back home in Bay St. Louis by Monday afternoon. "Alright, Honey, I know you have to get going too. We're so proud of you." Katherine embraced her son. "Come home as soon as you can tomorrow. You must be exhausted."

"No I feel fine, Mom. I will. As soon as I pack and clean up the apartment tomorrow, I'll be on my way home."

"Do you need any money? Tom expressed his love in a more fatherly way. "Be careful on the road tomorrow."

"No. Yes." John seemed a little anxious. "I mean no I don't need any money, and yes I'll be careful. He paused for a moment and took a breath. "By the way, Mom, Dad, there is someone I want you to meet."

The young lady had been waiting patiently, unnoticed in the crowd, watching the family goodbyes. As John turned toward her, she stepped forward and extended her hand to Katherine.

"Hi, I'm Mary."

CHAPTER 3

Martin Feeny and Karen Burns woke up in each other's arms, but their morning breath and pounding headaches would not allow them to even think about any morning love-making. "Oh, Shit. Oh, my God. My head. Ahh. Ahhh. Somebody, kill me. Please, kill me." Feeny was not feeling well. His long black hair fell over his face, parted by a rather large nose.

"What the hell time is it?" Karen fumbled for her watch.

"I don't know. I don't care. Just kill me. Please. What the fuck hit me?"

"It might have been Jack Daniels." Karen pretended not to feel quite as bad as Feeny. "Don't you remember?"

"Jack Daniels? Who's Jack Daniels?" Feeny squinted trying to focus on Karen's beautiful bare ass moving toward the bathroom. She kept herself in great shape.

"Oh, I get it, Jack Daniels. That's pretty funny." Karen turned on the shower, as Feeny tried to sit up in the bed. "Seriously, what happened to us?" He raised his voice so she could hear him over the shower and immediately regretted doing it, as his pounding head protested. "I don't even remember leaving John's place." He yawned. She turned off the shower, dried herself and reached for her toothbrush.

"As usual, you started acting like an asshole at John's and we had to leave." Moments later she emerged from the bathroom with a terrycloth towel tied above her firm breasts. It was not quite long enough. How could she look so good? He thought. Deeply regretting that he was in no condition to take advantage of the opportunity, Feeny was now considering suicide.

"John's place wasn't the only problem," She continued. "It was Cooter Brown's, after we left John's." Cooter Browns was the local watering hole, popular with the student crowd.

"Oh shit, that's right." Feeny remembered the crowd, the music, and the smell of stale beer. How could you let me go there?"

"I tried to get you back here, but you insisted we go. It seemed like everybody left on campus was at Cooter's, and you decided to drop your pants just for laughs." She was on a roll now. "You can be such a jerk, sometimes"

"Thank you. Thank you very much." Feeny tried his best Elvis impression, not knowing if she was really mad or really, really mad.

"And then Churchill, and Healy showed up. I was damn lucky to get you out of there at all." She was really, really mad. She let the towel drop from her perfect body and pulled on some sweat pants. "I'm going for a run. Try to get your shit together so we can get some breakfast when I get back." She tied her last sneaker and was out the door.

"Yeah, okay, Hon." Feeny whimpered as she slammed the door. "We'll have some breakfast after you have your run." He buried his head with a pillow. "Run? Breakfast? Fuck."

CHAPTER 4

"Mrs. Margaret Simmons?"

"Yes." She was middle-aged, with graying hair and a sweet round grandmother's face.

"Mrs. Simmons, I'm Lieutenant Nance and this is Sergeant McCaffrey. We're with the Louisiana State Police. May we come in?" This was the hardest part of police work. Earlier that morning, the N.O.P.D. called to inform the State Police that there had been a murder, and the victim's family apparently lived in Baton Rouge. News traveled fast; and New Orleans wanted to make sure that the parents were informed. The two officers were both over six feet and looked very professional in their dark business suites.

"Yes, of course. Is there a problem?" Margaret nervously continued to wipe her dry hands on her apron.

"I'm afraid it's about your daughter, Mrs. Simmons. Is your husband at home?" McCaffrey asked.

"No. He's playing golf. What about Mary? Is she all right? I am expecting her home any minute now. She is all right, isn't she?" Her heart was beginning to pound.

"Mrs. Simmons," Nance stepped forward. "your daughter was killed last night." The message was so brief. The words - so hard and cruel. Their meaning—so devastating. She stopped wiping her hands, and stood frozen, as her mind tried to process it all. She forced an uncertain smile, hoping that the encounter might be some terrible sick joke.

"That can not be true. That is not true. We were with her yesterday. She graduated from Law School. She's going to be a lawyer." The smile faded into desperation, as the officers remained silent. "Mary is very smart. She's going to be a lawyer." Still, no reaction. "Oh, God. Oh, God, no." She began to shake uncontrollably. "Oh, my God, no." Nance reached out and caught her just as her legs began to buckle under the tremendous weight he had laid upon her.

"Mrs. Simmons, we need to contact your husband. Can you tell us where we can find him?" He felt her begin to stiffen.

"Oh, my God. Bob. You can't tell Bob. You can't tell him this. It will kill him." She seemed to find strength in wanting to spare her husband from this terrible news. "I have to be with him. He's at the club. He plays golf on Mondays". Now her mind was racing. "We have to find him, and I have to tell him. I have to tell him about Mary." She began to look for a sweater, not really knowing why or what she would do next.

As the three approached the front door, the Buick pulled into the driveway. Her husband stepped out. She watched him approach, but she could not move to greet him. He waved as he started up the walk. "Hi, Honey, decided not to play. Too damn hot. Did Mary get home yet?" He walked up the stairs and kissed her on the cheek. The police officers politely stepped back into the house. "What's going on here? Gentlemen, I'm Bob Simmons. Can I help you with something?"

"Bob, they're with the police. Mary's been hurt. Why don't we sit down?" Her husband was a good man and a wonderful husband and father. He was big and strong, and his face portrayed the straightforward honesty for which he was known. He loved Margaret very much, but his daughter, his only child, Mary was his life. He adored her from the day she was born. She took her first steps into his arms. He taught her to ride her bicycle. He cried when he had to scold her. He worried about her through adolescences. He cheered when she gave the valedictorian speech in high school. He drove her to college. He showed her off whenever he could without embarrassing her. He was proud of Mary's outstanding work in college, which led to a full scholarship to Tulane Law School. And yesterday, in the New Orleans Super Dome, the dreams they shared had all come true.

"Hurt? What do you mean hurt? Is she here?"

"Mr. Simmons," Lieutenant Nance started.

"No, I'll tell him." Margaret, tears now running down her face, took her husband's hands in hers. "Oh, Bob, Mary's gone." He pushed her back to arms lengths, searching for meaning in her face.

"What are you saying?" His face flushed.

"Mr. Simmons, Your daughter was killed last night in New Orleans." Nance knew of no easy way to say it. Simmons turned his six-foot body slowly toward the Lieutenant, his face contorted with confusion, pain and anger. He pointed his finger at Nance and exploded.

"You shut up. Just shut up. I want you out of my house. Now. Mary is coming home today. That's why I came home early. She's going to be home soon, and I don't want you here. Get out. Both of you, get out of my house." Like a wounded animal, Bob did not know were to put himself. He began to stomp around the house, turning first to the living room. Then he walked toward the kitchen, and quickly did an about face and reentered the front hall where the other three stood motionless. He could not seem to ease his pain. "This has got to be some big mistake." He said pushing past the officers on his way back to the living room. Another about face, and he returned to the hall, and stood eye to eye with Nance. "How can you be sure? You can't be sure. Right?" He paused, waiting for the answer he would not hear. "Are you sure?" he pleaded. With each question, Bob's tone of voice went from anger to hope and finally to despair.

"Mr. Simmons, McCaffrey responded, there appears to be no mistake, but you will have to go to New Orleans to make a positive identification. You are to contact a Sergeant Bell of the N.O.P.D." There was certain finality to McCaffrey's directive, and the big man felt the life begin to drain from his body. He thought of Margaret, and he turned to her. She was trembling, face wet with tears, now unable to speak - to breath. He reached for her and pulled her close to him, and he held her like he had not done in a long time. She buried her face in his chest and sobbed deep heart breaking sobs. The officers turned away, and choked back their own tears. Bob lifted his head, his spirit now broken. He had no more strength to resist.

"I'll call Sergeant Bell right away."

CHAPTER 5

Contrary to Sergeant Bell's promise, John was not allowed to make any calls. He had been taken to the Central Lock-up, behind the courthouse on Tulane Ave. It was a deplorable place - dirty and smelly with scores of New Orleans 's finest standing around doing nothing. A large calendar was tacked to the wall. Grease penciled X's kept track of the elapsed days. It was Monday, May 10, 1998.

"We have to process ya'll," said one obscenely fat black women, bulging out of a police uniform that was never intended to sustain such abuse. She took his shoes, belt, and wallet and left him sitting in a small room behind a locked steel door. The window had wire mesh running through it. His head was still pounding, but he was feeling a little better. He could not stop thinking about Mary.

Who did this terrible thing to her? He remembered finding her on the kitchen floor, and the horror of the scene. He did not recognize her at first. He wanted the body to be that of someone else. Someone he didn't know. She had been beaten terribly, and stabbed repeatedly. Then he saw the pearls that he had given her the night before. It was Mary.

He remembered running back to the bathroom to throw some cold water on his face. He had to clear his head. In the mirror he could see blood in the bathtub. His blood, he thought from the head wound, but he noticed something else in the tub and wiped the mirror for a better view. Turning suddenly away from the mirror he looked directly at the object. It was a carving knife from his kitchen, crusted with dried blood. He stumbled out of the bathroom and called 911, and waited for the police.

After arriving at the Lock-up, and going over his story again and again with Bell, John was left alone and now no one seemed interested in him or in what he had to say. He had spoken to no one during the last two hours. Through the wire mesh window, he could see a clock on a greasy paneled wall outside the room. Close to three o'clock, he had to talk to someone. What was going on out there? He had to call his parents. They were expecting him before dark. He did not want to worry them. Why were they holding him for so long? John approached the steel door and pounded on it. "Hey, is any body out there? Hello? Is somebody going to let me out of here? Hello?"

A detective approached the door and motioned for John to step back against a wooden table. He unlocked the door and stepped into the small room. He wore a soiled white shirt, yellowed at the armpits. His five-foot-eight body was more than fifty pounds over weight, causing his belt and waste band to flip inside out under his ample belly.

"What do you want, John? I'm Detective Breaux. You want something?"

"Yeah, well, for one thing, I want to get out of here. I want to know what's going on. I'd like to call my folks and let them know where I am. That's what I want, to start with." Breaux moved around the perimeter of the room and came up behind him. John stood still. The detective's manner made him very uneasy. "I see," said Breaux, gently putting his hands on John's shoulders. Then with a sudden violent shove he pushed him down into one of the two chairs at the table. "And what about Mary Simmons, John? Don't you want to know about her?" His words were sharp and measured. "**We** would. Do you feel like telling us about Mary, now?" John felt the fingers digging into his shoulders. The fat man had a strong grip.

"Sure, I want to know about Mary. I want to know what happened to her. But I told Sergeant Bell that I…"

"Shut the fuck up. I don't want to hear what you told Sergeant Bell. I want to hear what you did to that girl, and we're gonna stay here all fucking night until you're ready to tell us." John could not believe what he was hearing. He suddenly remembered being read the Miranda Rights. He remembered the handcuffs. How stupid he'd been. His head was clearing quickly, now. He wasn't being questioned anymore. These guys really thought he killed Mary.

"What are you talking about? I didn't do anything to her. I loved her"

"Yeah, you loved her, and you killed her. You know it, and we know it. So, why don't you cut the shit and tell us what happened?" The detective was now leaning over the table, in John's face, and spitting through his coffee stained teeth. The young man was suddenly stone sober. He fully realized now the seriousness of the trouble he was in, and his legal training told him that this was the last guy in the world that he should be talking to.

"I'm supposed to be able to make a phone call, and I want to talk to a lawyer." He wiped the spit from his face and pretended not to be intimidated. Breaux straighten up and hiked up his pants.

"Okay, Johnny-boy, we'll do it your way. You can make your phone call, and you get a fucking lawyer. You're gonna need one, because your ass is gonna be mine before we're done." He steamed out of the room and slammed the steel door behind him. John heard the lock click into place. He put his face in his hands and exhaled. Two minutes later, the door flew opened again. John jumped. Breaux was back with a telephone. He threw it on the table.

"You got one call, asshole."

CHAPTER 6

The phone rang in John's empty apartment. It was locked and sealed off as a crime scene. The call was coming from the Café Du Monde in the French Quarter. As always, the famous tourist spot was dusted with powered sugar giving the impression that a massive cocaine bust had just gone seriously array.

"Nobody's answering," Courtney Roberts informed Allison McKay as she shook the excess sugar from her beignet. The two agreed to stop for coffee one last time at their favorite New Orleans hangout before beginning their long drive to Florida. The girls had met on campus two years earlier. Although, at the time, Courtney was in the Law School and Allison was pursuing a bachelor's degree in business, they were delighted to find that they had actually lived only twenty miles apart back in Daytona. Since then they became good friends and roommates.

They had spent the morning packing and vacating the long, narrow, ginger bread, shotgun they shared on Calhoun Street. It was a cute little place, and, as the name suggested, you could fire a shotgun from the front door to the back door without hitting anything. They hated to leave it, but now they were ready to leave New Orleans, and get on with their lives. Before setting out, they wanted to say good-bye to John and

Mary. They all had a great time the night before, and Courtney especially wanted to stay in touch with her classmates.

She was also anxious to make sure that everything was all right. There was a lot of drinking last night, and some stupid things were said and done. John got very drunk and a little carried away when telling the girls how much he loved them and how he was going to miss them. Mary was a good sport, but she did not appreciate his uncharacteristic behavior. She was embarrassed, as she watched this sloppy drunk, who she thought she loved, coming on to each of her friends. She had not seen this side of him before. She did not like it, and she let him know it.

Then things got worse when Martin Feeny, who was also way beyond his limit, tried to make a move on Mary, and ended up with his hands all over her. His girlfriend Karen got upset and dragged him out of the party at about one o'clock in the morning.

"You're acting like an asshole," she could be heard saying while pushing him out the door. Courtney and Allison helped Mary put John to bed at about one thirty and offered to help clean up the apartment, but Mary would have none of it.

"No, I want to leave this mess for Lover Boy to clean up in the morning." She said, and with that the three girls left the apartment, and locked the door, leaving the key under the rubber mat, as was their custom. Courtney and Allison walked Mary to her car, and the three said goodnight.

"So there's nobody at Mary's place, and John's not home either." Allison correctly summarized. "Maybe they got together for breakfast somewhere."

"But why don't they answer their cells?" Courtney wondered out loud. She was less concerned about Karen and Feeny. Feeny was a classmate, but not really a close friend. She had met him through John, and they all had a lot of fun together during the last two years, but without John present, she always felt a little uncomfortable being with Feeny. It was a little like the Seinfield episode when Elaine and George discover they have little in common without Jerry, but with Feeny, it was not quite so funny. He managed to graduate somehow, but Courtney could not understand what he and John had in common. John was tall and handsome, smart, and a classy guy, not withstanding last night. Feeny was kind of a bum, never well dressed or clean shaven, always first with an off colored joke, and always the last to take out his wallet.

Karen was another story. She was Allison's classmate and friend. Courtney did not like her very much, but for Allison's sake she was always gracious and willing to suffer through Karen's company, which she found to be boring and pretentious. Courtney would not miss her asinine cheek kiss whenever they met. Karen loved hanging out with the law students and took advantage of every opportunity to do so.

It was through Courtney, Allison and John that Karen met Feeny, and since then the two had carried on a not too discreet relationship. Courtney felt that Karen was using Allison and probably Feeny, as well, for her own purposes.

As for Dave Churchill and Patrick Healy, they were the guys that were always sort of just there. They were John's buddies and seemed to be available whenever the group went out. Just good friends, was the way Courtney and Allison described them.

But Churchill, along with half the other men on campus, was in love with Mary, and although she had no such interest in him, and made that clear, he promised that some day he would sweep her off her feet and steel her from John. It was all in good fun and somehow, whenever they all got together, which was frequently, the chemistry within the group seemed to work, and they usually had a good time.

"Oh well, its not like we'll never talk to them again." Allison said.

"I guess you're right," Courtney conceded. "It's getting late. We better get going. I'll drive as far as Biloxi." The girls walked down Decatur Street toward the French Market where they had parked in a hard to find legal space. Before going to their car, Allison insisted that they make a detour through the French Market to pick-up a half dozen warm pralines from Loretta's. Loretta made the best pralines in New Orleans, always fresh, warm, soft, and filled with pecans. Six of the sweet and creamy delights would last them all the way to Florida.

Before leaving, Courtney tried Mary's cell phone one more time. The voice mail answered. She waited for the beep. "Hey, Hon, been trying to reach you all morning. Hope you got home okay and everything is cool with you and Lover Boy. Sorry about last night. He didn't mean anything. He loves you a lot and would never do anything to hurt you. Believe me. I know. I'll tell you how when I talk to you. Al and I are heading out. Call you from Daytona. Bye. Love ya."

CHAPTER 7

It was quarter past one on Monday afternoon, when Patrick Healy thought he heard someone at his Magazine Street apartment door. He opened one eye and looked at the clock on the table beside the couch, where he had spent the night.

"Oh shit, one-fifteen." He rose up on one elbow and wiped his eyes. As he sat on the edge of the couch in his boxer shorts, shaking the cob-webs from his head, he listened again. Yes, there was someone knocking at his front door. He grabbed a pair of shorts and stumbled his way to the door. His two hundred and thirty pounds were not easy to move gracefully. He put both feet through the same leg of his shorts and nearly killed himself trying to get free. "Coming. I'm coming. Hang on." Finally, zipping up his shorts, he opened the door and blocked his eyes from the bright mid-day sun. Two black silhouettes filled the doorway. Healy squinted. "Can I help you?" He said.

"Are you David Churchill?" One of the men asked.

"No, I'm David's roommate, Patrick Healy. Who are you guys?"

"Mr. Healy we're with the N.O.P.D. I'm Detective Rochambeau. This is Detective Menard." Both held up I.D. wallets. "Can we come in?" They asked, pushing their way into the room, before Patrick could answer.

"Ah, yeah sure. I guess. Excuse the mess." Healy said, lifting one of the shades to let in the daylight. He looked around at the disorder of the three-room apartment. Ashtrays overflowed, cloths were draped over make shift furniture, and empty beer cans were everywhere. "We had a late night last night. Haven't had a chance to tidy up."

"Where is Mr. Churchill right now?" Detective Menard asked as he looked around the typical bachelors quarters.

"Ah, David? He's in n n n," Healy hesitated as he walked across the room to the bedroom and looked in. "Ah, no he isn't. I thought he might have been still sleeping. Guess he left before I woke up."

"Do you know where he might be?" Rochambeau asked.

"Ah, actually, no. We were both going to pack up and leave today. We graduated yesterday and did a little celebrating last night. Can you tell me what this is about?"

"Where were you last night Mr. Healy?" Menard asked.

"Well, like I said there were several of us who had dinner, and then we returned to a friend's place for a while, and after that Dave and I went to Cooter Browns. That's a bar at the end of St.Charles."

"And what time did you leave Cooter Browns?" Rochambeau asked.

"I left before two-thirty. I'm not sure when Dave left. I guess I was asleep when he got in. I don't know where he is now. Maybe he went home." Rochambeau took out a note pad.

"And where is his home? Do you know?"

"No, not actually. I know he lives in Shreveport, but I don't know where."

"Mr. Healy where were you before you went to Cooter Browns?" Menard seemed to want to move the questioning along.

"Well, as I said, we had dinner in the Quarter, and then went back to John Steven's apartment. We had a few beers there and David and I left for Cooters."

"Who was with you at Stevens' place?" Rochambeau asked as he continued to walk around the apartment.

"Okay. Let's see," Patrick said, rubbing his face briskly with both hands. "There was John and Mary, his girlfriend. There was Karen Burns and Martin Feeny, and two other girls, Allison McKay and Courtney Roberts, and me and Dave. Is there some kind of problem?"

Rochambeau ignored the question. "So when you and Churchill left the party who was there? "

"All of them. Everybody I just told you. The party was getting a little out of hand so Dave and I split."

"What do you mean, out of hand?" Menard took interest.

"Oh, you know, dumb shit. We all had a lot to drink. John and Marty started fooling with the girls. Nothing serious. Just kidding around. Mary got upset with John. Karen got really pissed with Marty, and it seemed like a good time to leave."

"So they were all there when you and Churchill left?"

"Right. Can you tell me what's going on?" Healy was growing a little impatient.

"Mary Simmons was killed last night sometime after one o'clock, at the Stevens' apartment." Rochambeau looked into Healy's eyes for his reaction to the news."

"Holy shit." Healy dropped down on the couch. "Mary? No, don't tell me that. Everybody loved Mary. Jesus."

"Can you think of anything that can help us out with this, Patrick?" Detective Menard approached him. Healy was still stunned by the news.

"No, other than what I told you. But she was fine when we left. John was with her. What about the others? What did they say? Jesus, wait ' til Church hears this." Rochambeau assumed his best police posture.

"Mr. Healy, we would appreciate it if you did not discuss this with anyone. We will probably want to talk to you again. Do you understand?"

"Yes, yes of course." Healy was visibly shaken, now. "But, I was planning on going home to Slidell today. Is that alright?"

"As long as we have an address and number so we can get in touch with you, you can leave" Detective Menard advised. The detectives let themselves out leaving Healy sitting on the couch still dazed. He wanted desperately to call someone, John especially. What about John? John had to know about it. Was he all right? He must be feeling awful. How could Mary be killed in John's apartment? Healy had to find out what had happened. Where the hell was Churchill at a time like this?

CHAPTER 8

John stared at the phone, wondering how he could break this news to his parents. They were expecting him home by now. He was already late. He knew they'd be worried. They always worried even though he was twenty-five years old. He reached for the phone, took a deep breath, and dialed. It rang three times, before someone answered.

"Hello." It was his mother.

"Hello, Mom, this is John, is Dad there?"

"John, where are you? We thought you would be home by now. Is there a problem?"

"Ah, I'm running a little late, Mom. Is Dad there?" He couldn't begin to explain this mess to his mother.

"Yes, your father is right here. He's been waiting for you. What time will you be home?" She persisted.

"Mom, can you put Dad on? I need to ask him something." John did not want to lie to his mother. This was news that his father would have to break to her.

"Yes, of course. Here he is." She gave Tom a puzzled look as she handed him the phone.

"Hello, John." His dad took the phone, "Where are you son? Your Mom's been worried."

"Dad, I'm in trouble." John had learned a long time ago that his father was the first one to turn to when he had a problem.

"What's the matter, son? Where are you?"

"I'm in the New Orleans Police Station, Dad. They have me under arrest. They think I killed Mary."

Tom Stevens moved the phone to his other ear as he tried to process the words in his mind; police station, arrest, killed Mary. "Wait a minute, John. Wait a minute. Slow down. I can't understand you." He looked at Katherine.

"Dad, it's a mistake, but I don't know what happened." He didn't know how to tell his farther how stupid he had been.

"Okay, Son. Take it easy. Start from the beginning." Tom tried to calm his son while not wanting to alarm his wife.

For fifteen minutes John rambled on incoherently. "They had dinner. They went to Bourbon Street....the streetcar ride....drinking....got sick....banged his head...the police...Mary's dead." Tom let him go on uninterrupted, still trying to understand.

"John, you have to slow down. He finally had to interrupt him. "I can't follow you."

"I know I was stupid, Dad. I had too much to drink, but I didn't kill her. I couldn't. I would never hurt her." He stopped. Tom held the receiver frozen to his face. This was the kind of phone call that every parent dreaded, and prayed would never come. Did he understand what he had just heard? His son was being held for murder. His son, who the day before had graduated from law school, was being held for the murder of his girlfriend. How could this be happening? How could such a wonder-ful thing turn into this nightmare?

"John, now you listen to me. Everything is going to be all right. I know its some kind of mistake. Don't worry. I'll leave for New Orleans right away. You hang in there. It will take me about an hour. " He looked anxiously at his watch. " I'll come down there and we'll get this straight-ened out." He wanted to sound as positive as he could for John's sake, but also for Katherine who had not moved since handing him the phone. As for himself, Tom had no confidence in what he was saying. Neither he, nor any member of the family had ever been in any real trouble before, certainly nothing of this magnitude.

"Tom, what is it?" Katherine, afraid to ask, could be silent no longer. "What's going on" She tried to read the expression on her husband's face. He put his hand up, waving off her questions.

"Do you understand me, John?" He tried to give his son some assur-ance. "It will be all right. We'll do whatever we have to do. You just wait there. I'll be there as soon as I can."

"Alright, Dad, I'll wait." As he hung up the phone he looked around the locked room and realized what a stupid answer that was. He wasn't going anywhere.

The first thing Tom needed to do was to relieve some of Katherine's increasing concern. "Look, he's alright. That's the important thing. He's not hurt. I don't want you to worry. There's just been some terrible mis-take. That's all." Katherine approached him.

"What kind of mistake, Tom? Where is he?"

"He's being held by the New Orleans Police. They're doing some kind of investigation. I'm going to go over there and see what I can do."

"What do you mean some kind of investigation? Has he done something?" She pressed him.

"Katherine, listen." Tom tried to collect his thoughts. "Mary Simmons has been killed and they're holding John for questioning." He tried to make those two facts somehow fit together logically. "It is probably just routine. I'm going to go over there and pick him up."

"Oh, my God, Mary Simmons? Killed? But, that's impossible, Tom. We just met her. She was so beautiful." She remembered the pleasant surprise the day before. Her son was so proud to introduce his new girlfriend. "Oh, poor John. Tom, he must be so distraught. I'm going with you."

"No, I wish you wouldn't." He knew there was more to the story than he wanted her to know at this time. "There's probably going to be a lot paper work to take care of, and you're not going to be able to do anything that I can't do. I wish you would stay here. I'll call you as soon as I know anything"

"I'm coming." Tom knew the discussion was over. Katherine moved out of habit, to tidy up the kitchen, and prepared to leave.

The drive from Bay St. Louis to New Orleans usually took him about an hour, but Tom made it in about 45 minutes. He was anxious to get to his son, and equally intent on avoiding as many of Katherine's questions as possible. By five o'clock he had arrived at the N.O.P.D. Central Station. As Tom pulled into the nearest parking space, he did not notice the big Buick from Baton Rouge parked next to him. The car had been there most of the afternoon.

CHAPTER 9

The morgue was located in the cavernous underground of the gray granite block courthouse on Tulane Ave. It was in this building almost thirty years earlier where Attorney General Jim Garrison prosecuted Clay Shore for conspiracy to assassinate President John F. Kennedy. The cellar served as a parking garage for the judges and VIPs who worked in the courthouse. Restricted-use elevators took the judges to and from their private chambers, protecting them from the criminals and, sometimes, the lawyers who filled the courtrooms above. There were also a number of office operations in the cellar, which supported the courts, but did not merit the coveted space on the main levels of the impressive structure.

Bob and Margaret Simmons were being led along the soot darkened concrete walls by Sergeant Bell. They moved slowly past the evidence room, past the print shop and toward the destination, that neither wanted to reach.

As they approached the old wooden paneled door, the single word painted in black block letters on the frosted window sent a chill through Margaret: **MORGUE**. It was an ugly word - a word sounding like the collection of horrors that the room had seen over the years. Bell stopped outside. "Mrs. Simmons this is going to be very hard for you. It is not necessary for you to make the identification. Your husband can do this."

"I want to see my daughter." She said, adamantly. Bob nodded to Bell, and the Sergeant opened the door. A technician seemed to be waiting for them. He had obviously been through this exercise before.

"This way please." He gestured as though he was escorting them to their seats at the Sanger Theater. A stainless steel cart was set in the middle of a ceramic tile floor. The floor had been recently washed down with a strong smelling disinfectant. It was not completely dry, adding to the chill in the room. Bob put his arm around Margaret to support her, and himself. At the appropriate moment, the technician reached across the cart, lifted the sheet, and folded it down across Mary's chest.

"Oh my God, no o o." Margaret gasped. She turned away and covered her face with both hands. Bob stared at the lifeless form on the cart. Was this really his daughter? With her beautiful face, smashed and broken, there were deep purple bruises and cuts on her shoulders and neck. He would not let himself think of what lay beneath the sheet. Standing motionless as if in a dream state, he studied what was once his little girl. Whatever it is in the brain that allows us to shut out such atrocities, was now letting him see past the wounds and broken bones, so that he could remember her as he had last seen her. Less than twenty-four hours ago she was beautiful with her long blond hair flowing from under her cap, and over her black gown. She was glowing, so full of hopes and dreams, as she embraced him, and her mother. That was his daughter. The girl he remembered. A tear ran down his cheek, and suddenly, his chest heaved, releasing a long heavy sigh. There were no words to express the pain pounding in his broken heart.

"That is Mary." Bob said the hardest three words he had ever spoken. He turned away from the cart, took Margaret by the arm, and walked toward the door. Bell spoke softly,

"Y'all will have to come back to the station now. I hate to ask y'all to do this, but we do have to ask some questions and complete some paperwork. It's necessary." Bob nodded. Nothing mattered to him now. Whatever had to be done, made little difference to him. Mary was gone and suddenly his life didn't seem to make much sense any more. Margaret walked along side, hanging on to his arm. Whatever had they done to deserve this?

At the same time, Tom and Katherine Stevens were hurrying aimlessly through the hallways of the police station, looking for some clue that might help them find their son.

"Excuse me", Tom stopped the first person he saw. "I'm looking for my son, he's been arrested"

"Oh yeah. What he do?" Unmoved by the urgency in Tom's voice, the women spoke perfect Ebonics.

"We're not sure why he's being held. Someone was killed." Tom started to tell her what he knew.

"There's been a mistake." Katherine interrupted. "He doesn't belong here. We came to take him home."

"I see." said the women. "Y'all better follow me". She walked them back down the hall in the direction from which they had come. At the end of the hall, the door to the stairwell opened. Sergeant Bell held it for the tall man and his sobbing wife. Tom and Katherine stepped aside to let them pass. For a moment the two mothers' eyes met, unaware of the enormous burden they shared. This was not a place where either wanted to be. The policewoman directed Tom and Katherine to a small waiting room. The brown plastic covering the couch between matching armchairs was torn. A single lamp with no shade lit the room. A faded Mardi Gras poster hung on the wall - someone's idea of brightening up the windowless room.

"Y'all be better off waiting here," she said. "Im'ma find someone to talk to y'all." She left them alone, sitting silently, unable to talk to each other, and not wanting to share the terrible fears and images that were racing through their minds.

"It'll be all right, Katherine." Tom broke the silence trying unconvincingly to reassure her. After what seemed an eternity, the door opened and Detective Breaux entered the room.

"Mr. Simmons, Ma'am," He nodded toward Katherine. "I'm Detective Breaux, and I'm afraid, I have to tell you, your son is in a lot of trouble. He's been arrested and charged with murder."

Tom and Katherine hung on every word, as though they were listening to a surgeon explaining in technical medical terms that their son had undergone a serious operation and was being held in intensive care. They waited for the good news, but there was none. Katherine finally shook her head, not believing she had heard him correctly.

"What did you say?"

"It's true, Ma'am. You are not gonna to be able to see him tonight. I'm sorry." Breaux was not wasting any words. Twenty years of police work, with the last seven in homicide, had hardened him to the emotions of normal people. This was New Orleans, where every morning the local newscaster read the casualty report of those killed in the streets of fun city. Most of the killing was drug related, blacks killing blacks in the deplorable public housing projects with deceptive names like St. Thomas and Desire, where dealers made a living taking advantage of the weaknesses of their less fortunate brothers and sisters. The Stevens case was unusual. Not the kind he was accustomed to. Rich white kids, with the best educations killing each other. He did not understand this kind of crime, and he had no tolerance for it.

"Now wait just a minute." Tom stood up. "We just drove sixty miles to see our son. If he's in trouble we need to talk to him." Tom could feel himself begin to shake. He was not accustomed to talking to a police officer in this way.

"That's impossible, Mr. Stevens. Best thing I can tell you is to find the best lawyer you can. Your son is gonna need one." Katherine waited for Tom to insist on something, but the hard facts of the situation were beginning to sink into his head. He knew there was nothing else they could do, at this time. "This is my number." Breaux said, extending a business card to Tom. "Call me tomorrow. I'll tell you where we're at." He turned for the door and left them staring at the card, totally perplexed. Katherine was devastated. For the first time in their lives they were powerless to help one of their children. What could they do to stop this terrible thing?

CHAPTER 10

The six o'clock news was all over the story.

"A Tulane Law School graduate was found brutally slain in the apartment of her boy friend early this morning." The young brunette, reading the story, tried her best to appear sincerely concerned. "The twenty-five year old woman has been identified as Mary Ellen Simmons of Baton Rouge. The boy friend and fellow graduate, John Stevens, is being held in connection with the murder."

A camera zoomed in on the apartment building, still encircled by yellow crime scene tape. A gray haired, on-the-scene, reporter stepped into the frame.

"Early police reports confirm that something went terrible wrong in this apartment building early this morning, when eight young graduates came together to celebrate. The camera panned. "For one of those graduates, Mary Ellen Simmons, the party would be her last."

The newscast went on to give details of Mary's background, and her academic achievements. A graduation picture of John Stevens now filled the TV screen.

"According to police sources, Ms. Simmons and this man, John Stevens, now in police custody, argued violently throughout the evening in front of witnesses who attended the party. It was sometime after the party broke up that Ms. Simmons was killed."

"Jesus Christ, that's bullshit." Martin Feeny was livid. "John could never do anything like that." He and Karen had been glued to the TV set since about three o'clock when two detectives banged on their door and interrupted an afternoon nap. "Where did they get that shit?" He went on. "Christ we were there. There was no violent fucking argument."

"Shut up. Shut up. Will you?" Karen sitting crossed legged in front of the TV waved her hand in his face as she watched the news. "I'm trying to listen to this." All afternoon they had been talking about Mary and John. How could Mary Simmons be dead? It was awful. Nobody would hurt her—especially not John Stevens. It just didn't make sense. She not only excelled in academics, she was a beautiful person, who would do anything for anyone. She was into everything. She wrote for the Law Review. She volunteered. She was a student lawyer, licensed to practice in the Law Clinic. Somehow she found time for everything and everyone.

"Ah, c'mon, Karen. John's getting fucked and you know it." Feeny opened another beer.

"I don't know a damn thing and neither do you." She turned to face him. "We left. Remember? No, you probably don't remember." She turned back to the screen looking and listening for some clue as to what might have happened after they left the party.

"I remember. I remember that there was nothing going on in that apartment that would lead to this bullshit." Feeny was right about that, she thought. Certainly, neither of them had said anything to the police that could substantiate the newscast. Sure there was some arguing, but nothing serious. Everything was okay when they left. That's what they had said. That's how they left it with the police. Still, it was true. Neither of them really could say how the night ended in that apartment

"In other news today," The brunette was back on the screen. "Mayor Morial released a poll which he claims supports his conviction that the electorate would like to see him run for a third term."

Karen turned off the set and looked at Feeny. "Think about it Marty. We don't know what happened. Do we? We do know that John was drunk and Mary wasn't very happy, especially after he kissed me like that. Maybe they had a fight. Maybe he hit her. Maybe it was an accident." Marty took a sip of beer and looked at her, muddling over the possibilities in his mind.

"Ya Think?" He said, now realizing she was right.

"No, I don't think. All I'm saying is we don't know." She turned the TV back on, just as the telephone rang. She answered it. "Hello?"

"Karen?"

"Churchill, where are you?"

"I just got back to Shreveport. I left New Orleans at nine this morning. What the hell's going on? Is it true what I'm hearing on the news?"

"Is that Church? Give me the phone." Feeny was all worked up again. "Can you believe this shit?" He said without saying hello. "And they think John did it."

"I know. I know, Marty. I saw the news. So what's happening? I mean has anyone talked to you?" Churchill wanted the inside track.

"Hell yes, the cops have been here all afternoon talking to Karen and me. Didn't they talk to you?"

"No, not yet. I've been driving all day." Churchill paused. "Why would they want to talk to me?"

"Because you were there, man. They're probably going to talk to all of us." Marty speculated.

"But we left early, Patrick and I." Churchill sounded anxious. He was thin and wiry, with gold rim glasses that he constantly had to reset on his nose. He ran his hair through his disheveled blond hair. " Did they talk to Pat?"

"Don't know. Haven't heard from him." Feeny answered

"Christ, let me talk to Karen." Feeny passed the phone to Karen.

"Wants to talk to you."

"Yeah, Church?"

"So, what do you make of this. Who do think could have done it?" Churchill had proven to be a good cross-examiner in moot court at school.

"I was just telling Feeny I have no idea. Sure, none of us believes John could do it but we just don't know what happened. Right?" Karen waited for confirmation.

"You're right, Karen. You're absolutely right. Where are Courtney and Allison?"

Chapter 11

"I gotta pee." Courtney and Allison had been on the road for about forty-five minutes. They had not gotten far. Heavy traffic heading east had taken them only to the seven-mile causeway crossing over to Slidell, about thirty miles out of New Orleans. The girls were anxious to get home. They had not seen their folks in a while. Neither Allison's mother, nor Courtney's father could make the commencement exercises. Allison's mom lived alone. Her father was dead. Courtney's dad was out of the country on a business trip. Her folks had divorced six years earlier. Her mother had remarried and was busy raising a second family. Courtney and her father remained close, and both were disappointed when he was unable to attend the commencement. She lived with her dad, when in Daytona,

"Must be the coffee." Courtney said.

"I guess so." Allison was starting to squirm. "Can you stop somewhere?"

"You mean right here on the bridge? That will look cute." Courtney laughed. They were still tired from the night before and had driven most of the way without talking very much. Allison was playing a CD and thinking about having completed college, and the days that lay ahead for her. She was tired of school and anxious to be out in the real world making some money for her and her mother. She was not blessed with good looks and high intelligence, and everything seemed to come hard to Allison. She envied Courtney - stylish and beautiful. All her friend had to do was pass the Bar Exam and she would be on easy street. The Bar would not be a problem for her, either. Courtney did well at Tulane, graduating in the top ten percent of her class. Both she and Mary Simmons were top students. That's how they met. They were both involved with the Law Clinic, where the ambitious law students were actually sworn in to practice law on a limited basis. The Clinic worked with indigent people, some environmental issues, immigration cases, that kind of thing. Courtney and Mary worked together on a number of cases and they had become good friends.

Allison, on the other hand was happy to have graduated, but she knew she would have to get an MBA if she wanted to make it in the business world. She had to work hard for her grades, and the idea of going back to school gave her a headache. She was reminded of her immediate problem.

"Courtney, can you drive a little faster, pleeeease."

"Okay, okay, hold on." Courtney looked at the speedometer. "I'll kick it up a couple of notches, as Emeril would say. "I think there's a restaurant just up the road." She too had been daydreaming but she was still thinking about last night. She hoped that Mary and John were okay. They were both going home today, but they certainly did not intend to say goodbye to each other. The two had met, according to John, while jogging in Audubon Park. Mary was tying a shoelace and he stopped to see if she was okay. John said it was just fate, and love at first sight.

Mary had another version of the story that she shared in strict confidence with Courtney.

According to Mary, she had seen John at a lecture series and became very interested in him. Their meeting was far from fate. Mary found out that John jogged regularly in the park and she orchestrated their chance meeting right down to the broken shoelace. Naively, John was amazed to find how much they had in common and was delighted when Mary agreed to have lunch with him. They'd been together ever since. Mary would kill Courtney if she ever told him the real story.

"If you don't stop this car, I'm gonna pee my pants" Allison was getting serious. Courtney loved both John and Mary, and she knew they would be perfect together. That's why she hoped that the silly incident of the night before had blown over. She wanted so much to put Mary at ease, and she knew she could if only John had not sworn her to secrecy, also. A week before graduation, John had confided in her that he intended to ask Mary to marry him. He was so much in love with her that he had impulsively bought an engagement ring, and he had asked Courtney to hold the ring for him. He planned to wait until the excitement of graduation was over, when he and Mary could get to know their respective families better. Courtney had intended to return the ring to him last night, but was afraid that in his condition, he might lose it. Her plan now was to drop the ring off at his home in Bay St. Louis, which was not far out of the way. She had wrapped the ring box in a plain brown wrapper, addressed it, and marked it confidential, in case John was not home.

"There it is." Courtney spotted a Waffle House and pulled in.

"Oh, thank God." Allison said, jumping out of the car before it stopped. A few minutes later, She returned with two diet cokes, and passed one to Mary as she pulled into traffic.

Neither of the girls saw the black Ford Expedition that seemed to come from nowhere. It plowed into Courtney's 1992 Toyota Cressida and spun the car around three times before it flipped over and skidded to an upside down stop. The impact crushed the driver's side, and the first flip ripped the door off the passenger side. The car then seemed to disintegrate as it continued to flip and turn.

The Expedition's right front bumper and fender were badly damaged, but not enough to stop the truck. After pausing briefly to look back, the driver hit the accelerator and fled the scene continuing East. Behind him, the wreck laid upside down in the middle of the highway. Inside were Courtney and Allison - both secured by seat belts, and both dead.

CHAPTER 12

They spent the night in New Orleans at the Hampton Inn, but neither Tom nor Katherine could sleep. They had been over and over what John told his father, and the little bit of information that Detective Breaux provided. Tom could not reach Breaux by phone as he had suggested.

"What are we going to do, Tom? What can we do?" Katherine hoped that he had been able to sort out the options and come to some conclusion. He had.

"We're going to do what that Detective said. We're going to get him a lawyer as fast as we can, and see if we can get him out of there." Katherine took comfort in her husband's resolve, but this was all so alien to her family and their life style. The only time they needed a lawyer was last year when they decided to have a will drawn, not that they had that much. They just wanted to make sure that the kids would get what they had, if something should happen. She remembered working out a list of assets with the lawyer and coming to the conclusion that, with the equity in their home, they had a net worth of about $180,000. Of that amount, they had some mutual funds that had a value of about $30,000, about $10,000 in a short term CD, a 1997 Mercury Marquis, furniture, some jewelry and a few collectables that might be worth another five or six thousand. With four kids, they were not able to put away as much as they had hoped they would through the years. Fortunately, Tom had a good company pension that would keep bread on the table, when he retired in two years, and she and Tom also had insurance policies that they took out on each other, when they were married. After 38 years, the policies would each provide a death benefit of more than $500,000. Tom had been studying the phone book since he had gotten out of bed.

"From what I can determine," he said "this guy Daniel Hingle seems to be the biggest criminal lawyer in New Orleans. At least he's got the biggest advertisement." She looked concerned.

"Oh, Tom, is this something we should be doing out of the yellow pages?"

"No, probably not, but, frankly, I don't know who to call. I'm sure this guy will be able to tell us what were dealing with, and what we need to do to get John out. Time is important right now, and we have to move quickly." Tom's voice was conveying the urgency that Katherine felt.

"Yes I suppose you're right." She concurred, as he picked up the phone and began to dial.

"Hello, can I speak to Mr. Daniel Hingle please?" He asked, with as much authority as he could muster.

"Who's calling please?" Her voice sounded like a cloths pin was pinching her nose.

"My name is Tom Stevens."

"One moment, please."

Tom heard music. She came back. " Hingle, Barrone and Associates. Can I help you?"

"Tom rolled his eyes. Yes, you can help me. I was holding for Mr. Hingle. I"

"One moment, please"

More music. He turned to Katherine. "Got me on hold."

The voice came back. "I'm sorry, can I help you?"

"Look, you can't help me unless you stop answering the damn phone for a few minutes and talk to me." His years on the road had left him with little patience for corporate front desks.

"How may I help you, sir?" He had her attention.

"I need to talk with Mr. Hingle." Tom was trying to control his frustration.

"Mr. Hingle is not in this office." The voice was mechanical.

"Well where the hell is he? This is his phone number." Tom's blood pressure was starting to climb.

"Sir, we have two offices. Mr. Hingle is in the Metairie office today. Would you like to speak with an associate?"

"I'll speak with anyone, who can help me." He said.

"One moment, please." The phone clicked. Now, Frank Sinatra was singing.

"You're flying high in April and shot down in May."

How ironic, he thought. "Hello, this is William Barrone, can I help you?"

"Mr. Barrone, my name is Tom Stevens. My son has been arrested and charged with murder. Can you help us?" He had no time for small talk. There was a pause on the other end. "Hello, are you there?" Tom asked.

"Ah, yes, Mr. Stevens, I'm here. Just getting a note pad. I heard about you son's problem on the news. Where are you calling from?"

"My wife and I are here in New Orleans, at the Hampton Inn. Is there some way we can meet with you today, this morning? We've been here since last night. They won't even let us see our son." Tom did not want to lose any more time.

"Mr. Stevens, I'm going to set up a meeting for you with Mr. Hingle. I'm sure he will want to discuss your case with you, personally. It will have to be this afternoon. Is two o'clock good for you?" Tom agreed to the meeting, which was to take place in Hingle's office on Carondolet Street. He and Katherine then freshened up as best they could with the few complimentary toiletries that the Hampton Inn had provided for their unexpected stay. They proceeded to the fourth floor where a breakfast buffet was laid out for hotel guests. It was nine-thirty.

The dining room was very pleasant and comfortable. Businessmen read their morning Times Picayune, while drinking coffee and eating toasted bagels. Children helped themselves to the breakfast cereal bar, and hotel staff provided cheerful and efficient service. As Tom and Katherine poured some coffee and looked for an empty table, they could not help but notice that most eyes in the room were fixed on the several TV sets that were bracketed to the ceiling. Expecting to see another disturbing newscast about their son, they reluctantly turned their attention to the screen above their heads. The news was not about John. It was a bulletin concerning a terrible accident that had claimed the lives of two young women the day before.

"The young women were recent graduates of Tulane University en route to their homes in Florida." The reporter read. "Police are asking anyone who may have information about this tragic hit and run to come forward."

"My God, Tom," Katherine could not take anymore bad news. It had been two years since she sustained a mild heart attack. She had fully recovered but the events of the last few days had been extremely stressful. "What is happening? Is the world going crazy?"

CHAPTER 13

This was one of the worst traffic fatalities that the Slidell Police had ever recorded. The coroner said that the girls were probably killed on impact. Certainly, Courtney was. Allison may have survived the initial impact, but her body had sustained such trauma from the car's twisting and turning that she was also dead when the vehicle came to rest. The police were now picking up the pieces and trying to determine the facts surrounding what they could only call a fatal hit and run accident.

There were a number of witnesses who had been in the restaurant as Courtney pulled into traffic, but their statements were all the same. Everything had happened so fast. By the time they looked up from their meals the Toyota was in the air. A number of vehicles traveling behind the accident pulled off the road into the restaurant parking lot, but few of the drivers could add anything to the information that the police had already collected. One thing seemed certain. The girls were hit by a large black vehicle that stopped momentarily, and then drove off.

The first officers on the scene immediately sent out a description of the hit and run vehicle. Louisiana and Mississippi State Police along with local departments from Slidel to Biloxi were put on alert. Within the hour, the vehicle was spotted in a truck stop about twenty miles east from the scene. The radiator of the Ford Expedition had been badly damaged and the vehicle was over heating. There was no one in or around the vehicle.

State and local police vehicles filled the truck stop within minutes of the alert. State Police helicopters flew overhead, as ground troops encircled the restaurant. Several police officers, with guns drawn, entered the building while others began to organize a search of the marshy woods along the highway. There were about twenty customers in the restaurant, and several workers behind the counter.

"Everyone, just stay where you are. If you're sitting, sit. If you're standing do not move." State Police Detective, Don Crawford, with his badge held high seemed to be the officer in charge. "We need your cooperation, folks, and we'll get you on your way as soon as possible." Systematically the police moved throughout the restaurant sectioning it off into smaller quadrants. Working in teams, the police identified the patrons and escorted them to their vehicles, where licenses and registrations where checked. The customers were questioned as to any information they might have about the black vehicle, and then allowed to leave. As the restaurant was vacated, the workers were also questioned. None of them seemed to know who might have arrived at the truck stop in the black vehicle.

Outside other detectives were carefully going over the hit and run truck. It was a Ford Expedition, 1998. There was neither a registration nor any other documentation in the glove compartment or other storage areas within the vehicle. A tow truck was standing by to remove the vehicle to the nearest state police garage, where it could be examined more closely.

With only a few customers remaining in the building, Crawford looked around the room. In the corner sat a family with three young kids halfway through their waffles and sausages. An elderly couple sat nervously by the kitchen door unable to eat. A couple of truck drivers, sitting sideways with their backs against the wall, enjoyed coffee and cigarettes as they watched the police work, somewhat amused by the whole operation. None seemed likely to own the Expedition. Crawford turned to join the police officers, who had secured the vehicle, when his eye caught the small sign. There was one word and an arrow hand carved into a piece of cypress wood, **RESTROOMS**. He signaled to the young trooper who was interviewing the elderly couple. Both men approached the sign.

Within a small hallway was a door leading to the ladies room and directly across, was a door marked **GENTS**. Crawford opened the door to the ladies room and motioned for the trooper to watch the other door. He crouched down and looked under the stalls. He saw nothing. He stood up and moved cautiously along the stalls; opening each one just enough to determine that it was empty. He motioned to the trooper, that the room was cleared, and approached the men's room door. Following the same procedure, his eyes went from stall to stall. In the last stall he saw the shoes. He pointed, to the corner and the young trooper took cover behind a partition.

"Open the stall slowly and come out with your hands behind your head." Crawford's voice was calm, slow, and deliberate. He waited. Nothing. He looked at the young trooper, and gave him a puzzled look. "I'm talking to you, asshole. You got ten seconds to get out of there." Still nothing. Crawford motioned for the trooper to cover him as he moved closer to the corner stall. When the moment seemed right, Crawford stepped in front of the stall and placed his right boot heel squarely on the rusted handle. The door exploded open, and all hell broke lose.

"No shoot. No shoot me, I no speak English. No English." He was screaming, hysterically, in a heavy middle-east accent. "No English. Please no shoot me." Crawford held his gun level at the pathetic sight, cowering in front of him. The man was trembling with his hands over his ears, expecting to hear the blast that would send him to back to Allah. "Please, please no shoot me. Was accident. Was accident. Please, please no shoot." He continued to scream, while huddled in the corner.

"Shut the fuck up." Crawford hollered unable to stand the racket coming from the stall. "Nobody's gonna shoot you." He spun the man around and pinned him against the sidewall. He was not armed.

"Please. Please. Was accident. Don't shoot me." He continued to scream hysterically as Crawford locked the cuffs behind his back.

"If you don't shut up, I will shoot you." He motioned to the trooper. "Take this camel jockey, asshole out of here. He's giving me a headache." The man had no identification that made any sense to the police. He had no driver's license, and either could not or would not properly identify himself. There was no doubt that he was the driver of the black Expedition, and he was able to make the police understand that he did not see the girls pull into traffic in time to stop. He could not help hitting their car. When he looked back to see what had happened, he panicked and fled. He was booked for hit and run, and jailed pending further processing.

CHAPTER 14

Hingle was impressive. With pinstriped suit, monogrammed cuffs, and a gold Rolex hanging loosely from his wrist, he displayed all the trappings of a man with a successful law practice. He was also considerably overweight, testifying to the fact that he had eaten more than his share of read beans and rice. It was two- thirty. He had already kept the Stevens waiting thirty minutes for the two o'clock meeting. At two thirty-one he made a grand entrance into the waiting room, and turned toward the front desk.

"Delores, no calls while I'm with the Stevens'. Hi folks, Dan Hingle." He extended his hand to Tom, and then to Katherine. It felt like a wet fish. "Let's go into the conference room where we won't be interrupted." He led Tom and Katherine down a carpeted hall to a large room that featured a twelve-foot solid teak conference table. Black leather chairs surrounded the table. Awards from various civic organizations, framed in gold, lined the walls. He took a compact cell phone from his vest pocket. "Tell Barrone to reschedule that deposition. See if we can do it tomorrow. Have a seat folks." He motioned for them to sit, while he took a seat at the opposite end of the table. Appearing to search for the right words, he paused long enough to make sure that he had their complete attention. "How old are you Mr. Stevens?" Tom was surprised by the question, but answered.

"I'm fifty-eight."

"And you Mrs. Stevens, about the same?" He assumed.

"Yes, fifty eight." She said. Hingle paused again. "We don't know why the things that happen to us in this life do. In my line of work, I see a lot of difficult cases. I see a lot of bad things happen to a lot of good people." Katherine was nodding her acquiescence, as Tom was growing anxious. "I am going to be very honest with you." He learned forward. "Your son is in a lot of trouble. Serious trouble."

"Mr. Hingle, we already know that." Tom leaned forward. "That's why we are here."

"I took the liberty of calling Chief Pendleton." He ignored Tom's impertinence. "He has confirmed that your son has been charged with second degree murder in connection with the death of his girl friend, a Miss Mary Simmons, which occurred after an argument between them last Sunday evening. He is being held without bail. He further informs me that there were witnesses to the argument and that there is physical evidence that irrefutably ties your son to the murder." He stopped to let the importance of his words sink in. "Now, I don't mean to alarm you unnecessarily. I am very good at what I do. But, if I am to represent your son in this matter, I want to be very direct and honest with you. We may have a long road ahead of us, and I want you to be prepared."

"But Mr. Hingle, John could not do this." Katherine could no longer remain silent.

"Mrs. Stevens that may or may not be true, but legally speaking, it is not important." He stood up and walked around the room. "What is important is that the prosecutor must prove that John killed this girl, and we must do everything in our power to establish reasonable doubt in the minds of the jurors, so that he will not be convicted"

"Wait a minute, wait a minute." Now Tom was on his feet. "Mr. Hingle aren't we getting a little ahead of ourselves here? We wanted to talk to you so that you could tell us how to proceed with this thing. I mean what do we need to do to get John out of jail, and then we can figure out what the next step is."

"Mr. Stevens, I've tried to convey the seriousness of this situation. There is no way to get your son out of jail until we get a bail hearing. Now, I'm prepared to do what I can to get that hearing set, as soon as possible; and I will represent John if you decide to retain this firm. But, I assure you, this is a matter that will require a lot of time and effort if we are to succeed. What's more," He went on. "if I am to commit the resources of this law firm to freeing your son, I will need a commitment from you to do what is necessary to prevail in this effort."

"All right, All right," Tom wanted to get on with it. "What do you need from us?"

"My fee is $175 per hour, and $250 per hour if we go to trial. In addition, you will be responsible for all expenses related to the case. I will require a $50,000 retainer up front." Hingle quoted the figure without the least bit of hesitation.

"$50,000?" Tom fell back in his seat. "Jesus, where are we going to get $50,000?" He looked Katherine. She reached over to him and said,

"Tom we'll get it. We have to get it. What else can we do?"

"All right, Mr. Hingle you're hired. It might take a few days to get you a check for the full amount. How much will you require to talk to John and get started?"

"That's quite all right Mr. Stevens." Hingle was now trying to show what a wonderful human being he could be. "A few days will be fine.

With your consent, I will move immediately to meet with John and try to get a bail hearing scheduled."

"Yes, yes of course, the sooner the better." Tom authorized Hingle to proceed immediately, and searched Katherine's face for some clue as to how they could ever handle this.

CHAPTER 15

Matt Stevens was pacing the floor in his Houston office, when the phone rang. Normally, Matt could maintain control in difficult situations. At thirty-five, he had worked his way up the corporate ladder, and was already in contention for a Vice Presidency in Houston's prestigious, Wilkins and Marrow Advertising Agency, where he had been employed for the last seven years. He had gotten the attention of the corporate inner circle five years earlier, when he landed an account for a major sports franchise, headquartered in the Houston area. Since then he had developed a reputation for having a great rapport with his clients, as well as an ability for grasping a simple idea and developing it into a clever advertising campaign. He was smart and talented. The promotion was important to him. He worked hard. He deserved it, and he wanted it. But this afternoon he was worried about news coming out of New Orleans. Something he could not control. He reached for the phone, hoping it was not a client.

"Hello, Matt Stevens."

"Matt this is Mike."

"Jesus, Mike, how are you?" He knew what his younger brother was calling about. "This thing is driving me nuts."

"Me too, Matt. I can't get it off my mind." Michael was hyperventilating. "How did you hear?"

"Dad called this afternoon. He said he was going to call you and Martha."

"Yeah, he did, but Matt, I heard it on the radio this morning while driving to work. Not that John was involved, but they were talking about the murder. It was awful. And then Dad calls and tells me John's in jail. Holy shit. We gotta get back there." He took a breath hoping that Matt had a better handle on the situation than he did.

"I'm not sure there's anything we can do, Mike. Mom and Dad have already hired a lawyer, and they have to wait and see what he says." He paused for Mike's reaction.

"Christ, Matt, we were just there. How could things get so screwed up so fast? Do you have any idea what happened?" Matt had been asking himself the same question all morning. He needed a plausible explanation. No one in the office had yet approached him, but he knew it was coming. First there would be the expressions of concern. Then the questions. Then the behind the back whispers. By the end of the week his brother's involvement in the New Orleans murder would be all over the building. His clients would, of course, get word. He needed to have some response that would mitigate the potential damage that this thing could cause.

"I don't know Mike. The cops don't charge you with murder, without some evidence." He reasoned.

"Matt," Mike shot back. "you can't think John had anything to do with this. Do you?"

"No of course not. I just can't figure out why he is being held. I mean, why John? Mom and Dad met the girl after we left on Sunday. He had a date with her that night, and the next day she's dead, and John's in jail. I don't know what the hell happened, but I do know it looks very bad." He paused. "It looks bad for all of us."

"Tell me about it. Kimberly is going ballistic." Kimberly was Michael's wife. She was from a very well to do Chicago family. Her father was a senior partner in Mike's company. He had brought Mike into the firm when he decided that Mike's software selling job was not sufficient to provide Kimberly with the life style she was accustomed to. "Her mother and father are throwing a fit."

"Hang on, will you, Mike? My other line is ringing." Matt pushed the hold button. "Hello."

"Matt, this is Martha."

"Martha," Matt rolled his eyes, not wanting to have the same conversation with his younger sister. "I got Mike on the other line."

"Matt, what are we going to do?" Martha started to cry. "What are they doing to John? Mom and Dad are a wreck. Dad called me. They're in New Orleans and they can't even see him."

"I know. I know, Martha. Don't cry I'm talking to Mike right now. Let me see if I can hook him in." Matt hit the conference line. "Mike, I got Martha."

"Martha," Mike said, "I was going to call you next."

"Oh Mike, isn't this terrible? Matt, we have to help Mom and Dad with this." She waited for a response.

"I was just telling Mike that I don't know what we can do at this point." Matt answered. "Seems to me we are all going to have to wait until we get more information. What do you think, Mike? "

"Well, there must be something we can do." Mike answered. "Maybe go to New Orleans and talk to the police, or something. You know - tell them John could never do anything like this."

"I'm worried about Mom." Martha interrupted. "This is going to be very hard on her."

"Look," Matt was back. "This is going to be hard on all of us, but we're not going to do any good running around telling the cops what a great guy John is. We need to wait for Dad to tell us what we can do."

"I guess your right Matt." Mike conceded. "I know Kimberly does not want me to go to New Orleans anyway."

"Well I'm going." Martha broke in. "Mom's going to need some support. I don't know what I can do, but I'm going. Kimberly is not telling me what to do."

"It's not like that, Martha," Mike broke in defending himself from her implication. "You have to understand her family is very upset over this."

"Her family?" Martha was getting hysterical. "What about our family?"

"Okay. Okay." Matt cut in. "Let's not come unglued here. Martha, if you can take the time from work, maybe it is a good idea for you to go and be with Mom. Mike and I will stay in touch with Dad, and as soon as he thinks we can be of some help, we'll go down there. How does that sound?" He waited for a response. "Martha? Mike?"

"Yeah, okay that sounds good to me." Mike spoke first.

"Fine. But, I'm going to get the first flight I can." Martha had collected herself. "I'm sorry, Mike, but this isn't about Kimberly's family."

"I know. I know." Mike answered. "Let's just leave it the way Matt said, and you be careful."

"I will, and I'll call you both when I get there. Okay?"

"Okay, Martha." Matt spoke. "And Mike's right, be very careful. Anything can happen in that city. We'll be waiting for your call." He was not really happy with her going to New Orleans, but he was not up to arguing with her. She hung up.

"Mike, you still there?"

"Yeah I'm still here. Like I need that shit, right?" He was still smarting from Martha's kick in the balls.

"She's upset. Forget about it." Matt had been refereeing little spats between his siblings since they were kids. "She needs to see Mom. Let her go. Dad will probably send her back on a return flight. What can she do?"

"Yeah, okay Matt. Listen, I gotta go. Let me know if you hear anything, will you?"

"Sure, Mike, and you too; let me know what you hear." They agreed to stay in touch and hung up. Matt looked out his eighteenth floor window. There were heavy black clouds developing on the horizon. A storm was coming.

CHAPTER 16

It was Wednesday morning, ten o'clock. John Stevens and Daniel Hingle sat across from each other, separated by an old wooden table crudely inscribed with *Life Sucks,* and hundreds of other equally inspirational words of comfort. There were bars on the door, and a police officer stood outside. John looked terrible. He was wearing an orange jump suit, several sizes too big, with OPP, for Orleans Parish Prison, stenciled across the front. He had not slept much since his arrest. He was exhausted, still trying to figure out what had happened to him; and he had not even begun to deal with the loss of Mary.

"John, I'm Daniel Hingle." Hingle introduced himself, sounding very much like his TV commercials. "Your Dad has retained me to see if we can get you out of this mess. I have spent a good part of Monday and all of yesterday trying to find out what they have. Now, I need to hear from you, but I want to make a few things very clear before you say anything. You are in serious trouble. You're being charged with second-degree murder. That's a mandatory life sentence in Louisiana. They claim you killed your girlfriend after a quarrel. There are witnesses who will testify to that quarrel. They have a weapon, with your prints on it. And, they have you at the scene." He looked into John's eyes, and shook his head up and down, affirming the seriousness of the situation.

"Look, Mr. Hingle", John interrupted.

"I'm not finished yet. Listen to what I say." Hingle did not like being interrupted. "Now, I want you to understand one thing, from here on out. I call the shots. I don't want you to do anything, without my approval. I don't want you to say anything to anyone, unless I say it's okay. Most importantly, I want the truth. There is no way that I can defend you unless I know everything you know about what happened in that apartment. Do you understand me?" John was growing restless with Hingle's pedantic and condescending attitude, but he was grateful that he was there, and he was anxious to talk to an ally.

"Yes, of course, I understand."

"Okay, now let's get started." Hingle took a tape recorder from his briefcase and hit the record button. He identified himself, stated the date and time, and named John as his client. "I want you to tell me about Mary Simmons." John paused before answering, remembering her face, her eyes, and her blonde hair. He leaned forward and looked directly at Hingle, as he spoke

"I loved, Mary Simmons. I was going to ask her to marry me. I even bought her a ring."

"Tell me how you met". Hingle looked at his watch. John talked about their chance meeting in Audubon Park, and then with great detail he narrated the last two months of school, when he and Mary did everything together, and found themselves falling in love. As John spoke, his memory returned him to those happier days.

"Did you have sex with her?" Hingles probe stung like a bee. The question was so abrupt and callous. It sounded dirty, and so alien to anything that he had ever shared with Mary, especially their love. He resisted answering, and let his mind continue to drift back to a special afternoon in May, when he and Mary spent most of the day studying for exams.

At about three in the afternoon, he suggested they go for a run to relieve some tension. Mary agreed. They changed into running clothes at school, and then headed across St. Charles Avenue to the park. It was a beautiful clear day, free of the oppressive New Orleans's humidity. They ran together through the zoo, stopping to catch their breath at the great ape exhibit. It was John's favorite. They stayed for a few minutes and watch the gorillas and orangutans. The apes in turn studied them, seemingly with much more interest and intelligence. After teasing John about one hairy female orangutan that was obviously interested in him, Mary ran off, laughing.

John chased after her and caught her at the sea lion exhibit. Young kids sat on the ascending concrete steps of a small amphitheater anxious for the afternoon show to get under way. Suddenly, without warning two large sea lions broke the surface of the enormous water tank and sent a tsunami into the crowd. The kids screamed with delight, and John and Mary, both too stunned to react, turned slowly toward each other. They were drenched from head to toe. Mary's long blonde hair was plastered against her face. The sleeves of her sweat-shirt hung down to her knees. She stood mouth open and speechless. John, unable to contain his laughter, said "oops" and began to run toward St. Charles Avenue.

"Oops? I'll kill you." She yelled, as she took up the chase. By the time they hit the avenue they were still laughing hysterically and still dripping wet. John made a joke about the tremendous sweat they had both worked up. Soon they were in the neighborhood of John's apartment and they agreed it would be a good idea to get some dry cloths. John took the key from under the mat and opened the door. He found a couple of beers in the fridge and opened one for Mary. They were both still feeling giddy. He told her to find something dry in his closet, while he headed for a quick shower.

He did not hear the bathroom door open, but he suddenly felt her presence in the room. She gently pulled back the shower curtain and stepped into the tub. He looked at her through the warm water running down his face. She was beautiful. The water splashed off his hard body to her soft curves. She stepped closer to him and pressed her breasts against him. With the soothing water washing over their naked bodies, they held each other. He pushed back her wet hair that had been so comical in the park. She smiled at him, and he kissed her lips. Nothing had ever felt so right, or so wonderful for either of them. He turned the water off and lifted her into his arms. He carried her, soaking wet, to the bed, and there they made love, long and hard, and beautiful love.

"Did you have sex with her?" Hingle's voice again shattered the memory. He was growing impatient with John's apparent lack of attention. "You better get used to these questions, because if I don't ask them, you can be damn sure the prosecutor will."

"Yes we had sex, but we loved each other. We respected each other."

"Did you ever hit her? Did you ever get rough with her while having sex?" Hingle persisted.

"Hell, no. I told you there was never anything like that." Now, John was getting angry.

"Alright, now I want you to tell me what happened that night."

John took a deep breath. How many times had he told this story? How many times had he racked his brain trying to fill in the missing pieces? "There were a number of us who decided to stay in New Orleans, after graduation, so that we could have dinner together and celebrate."

"How many? Who were they?"

John recited the names and continued. "We ate in the Quarter, an Italian place. After dinner we decided to walk off the meal. We had also finished several bottles of wine and needed some fresh air. We walked through the Quarter over to Bourbon Street."

Hingle interrupted again. "Did you make any stops on Bourbon Street? Did anyone see you there?"

"No. We bought some beers in the street, but we didn't go into any of the clubs. We had planned to go back to my place and hang out for a while." John was trying to focus on what followed.

"What time did you get back to your apartment?"

"It had to be ten-thirty, maybe eleven. I don't really know." John shook his head.

"John, these are extremely important questions." Hingle was in his face. " You have to try to remember as many details as possible."

"I know. I know. I'm trying to." John continued. "The reservation was for eight. It took about two hours to get served and finish the meal. We walked for about forty-five minutes, and took the St. Charles streetcar back to my place. That took a half hour. So, that would make it about quarter past eleven."

"So at eleven-fifteen you're all back at your place and everyone is fine." Hingle concluded.

"Well, not exactly." John shook his head. "Marty Feeny and I were doing Jack Daniels shots on the streetcar. He had a pint. And, I guess, with the wine and the beer and the Jack Daniels, by the time we got to the apartment we were pretty wasted."

"What do you mean?" Hingle leaned forward

"I don't know. Everybody started talking about not seeing each other for a while, and saying goodbye. And then the hugging and kissing shit started. I kissed Courtney and got a little carried away. Mary got really mad, and Courtney pushed me away. Then, I fell over the couch and landed on top of Karen. So, I started with Karen, but she didn't push me away. Then, Mary throws a glass of water at me; and I said something stupid to her."

"Where was Mary when she threw the water?"

"She was right there, in the kitchen." He was trying to remember. "Anyway, when Feeny, who's really cocked now, sees me on top of Karen, he gets pissed off and grabs Mary, and tries to kiss her. Mary shoves him, and he falls over the kitchen table, knocking beers bottles, potato chips and everything else onto the floor. Now, Karen gets ripped at Feeny, and pushes me off her, and I land on the floor. Next thing I remember, Karen is dragging Feeny out the door."

"Where were the other two guys? What are their names? Churchill and ah?" Hingle was trying to visualize the apartment.

"Healy. Patrick Healy. Ah, lets see, he and Churchill were just sitting in the living room drinking beer. When Karen started to raise hell, they just left." John shrugged.

"So, that left you and Mary and Courtney and the other girl, right?"

"Allison McKay"

"What?"

"Allison McKay that's her name. The other girl."

"Right." Hingle was pacing. "So then what happened?"

"I don't know."

"What do you mean, you don't know?"

"I don't know. I was lying on the floor. That's all I can remember. Next thing I know I'm in the bath tub, with a cut on my head, and feeling like I got hit by a train." John felt his head.

"What about the knife? Hingle looked at him. How did the knife get into the tub?"

"Jesus, I don't know. I don't even know how the hell I got into the tub."

"Okay, so you wake up, see the knife, then what?"

"No, not at first. I went to the kitchen and found Mary. Then I went back into the bathroom and saw the knife. That's when I called 911and waited for the police. They took about half hour to get there, and I told them the same thing I just told you." John leaned back in the chair.

"Did you touch the knife when you found it in the tub?" Hingle was speaking very slowly.

"No. I just left it there. But I did tell the police where it was when they showed up."

"John, I need to ask you this. Is it possible that you and Mary had a fight after you woke up, and you killed her with that knife?" Hingle was staring at him again.

"No. Hell, no. How could I do a thing like that and not remember it? I'd have to be out of my mind." Hingle stopped pacing, turned and looked directly at John.

"Yes, I guess you would."

CHAPTER 17

The bail hearing was set for Friday at ten in the morning. Hingle called Tom and Katherine, and Tom called Matt and Michael. Martha had been with them since Tuesday.

He told the boys that Hingle thought it would be helpful if the family made a strong appearance at the hearing. He also asked them to come to show their support for John. Matt said he would be there. Michael and Kimberly had made plans for a long weekend with her family, but Mike said he would cancel them if his father thought it was important for him to be there. Tom did.

Hingle met the family in the corridor outside the courtroom. Tom introduced Matt and Martha, and explained that Michael, who had not arrived, was running late.

"That's alright." Hingle said. "I'm glad you two could make it. Okay here' s what's going to happen in there. When John was arrested, the prosecutor asked that he be held without bail. John had nobody to object to that at the time, and the magistrate granted the request. With representation now, John has the right to ask for a hearing to reconsider bail. I submitted that request in writing as soon as you retained me. That got us to this hearing. Now, I'm going to ask that John be released on bail based on his background, and the stability of the family. The judge will take into consideration the fact that he's never been in trouble, and there shouldn't be any problem granting bail. You'll be required to post ten percent of the bail amount with some surety for the balance. That could be substantial. Are you prepared for that?"

"We've taken a line of credit on the house. We can raise about eighty thousand over your retainer." Tom was anxious. " Do you think that will be enough?"

"I can't say for sure. I'll do my best to keep it down. We better get inside, now." Martha looked at Matt, and pointed to her watch. She waited until Tom and Katherine were in the courtroom before asking what had been on her mind all morning.

"Where's Mike?"

"I don't know. Maybe he missed a plane." Matt did not want to get into this with Martha.

"Let's get inside."

The Judge presiding over the bail hearing would not be hearing the actual case, and Hingle felt confident that he would be receptive to setting a reasonable bail. His confidence faded a little when he glanced over to the prosecution table. Bradford Stern was thin and wiry with chisel sharp features. He loved his name, almost as much as he loved putting the bad guys in jail. He took no prisoners, and his conviction record was impressive. Hingle had already met with Stern to review the evidence against his client, and to determine if Stern might be inclined to discuss a deal. Stern made no such overture, and when Hingle suggested that he might be willing to plead the case out, Stern reminded Hingle that he had a weapon, motive, opportunity, and as far as he was concerned, this case was a slam-dunk. Hingle did not pursue it any further.

As Tom and Katherine took their seats behind the railing to the rear of the defense table, John was brought into the courtroom with his wrists shackled to his waste. Katherine gasped at the appearance of her son. Tom put his arm around her shoulder to comfort her, and to restrain her from going to him.

"Mr. Hingle, you requested this hearing, are you ready to proceed?" The judge looked down over the top of his Ben Franklin reading glasses.

"We are, Your Honor."

"Mr. Stern?"

"Of course, Your Honor."

"Proceed then, Mr. Hingle."

"Good morning, Your Honor." Hingle stood, buttoned his jacket and removed his glasses. "My client's family is present here today to support their son and brother. The Stevens Family has been a credit to the community. Mr. and Mrs. Stevens have lived a good life and they have raised a family that any of us would be proud of. Young John Stevens is a member of that family. Like the rest of the members, John has never been in any serious trouble. He has been an outstanding student, who has, within the last week, achieved his life long dream of graduating from Tulane Law School. Your Honor, we fully appreciate the seriousness of the crime with which this young man is being charged, but we also believe that when the evidence is heard the only conclusion will be that John Stevens is not responsible for it. I would ask the court to consider the fact that it was John Stevens who called the police upon discovering the body of the young women who he intended to marry. He had no motive for this horrendous act, nor did he have the capacity to carry it out. Mr. Stevens poses no threat to the community nor does his background suggest that he would make any attempt to flee. We ask that the court set the minimum bail possible in this case."

The judge turn toward the Prosecutor's table. "Mr. Stern what has the State to say in this matter?"

"Your Honor," Stern was already on his feet. "the evidence in this case will show that John Stevens brutally attacked and killed Mary Ellen Simmons, and that having so acted, he does indeed present a serious threat to the community. Further, we submit that the evidence against this defendant is so overwhelming that the possibility of flight, if he is given the opportunity, is very real and probable. The fact that Mr. Stevens has no criminal record does not in any way mitigate the seriousness of this crime. It was a vicious, cold-blooded act that destroyed a promising young life and left her family devastated. The people ask that bail be denied in this case, and that Mr. Stevens remain in custody to await trial."

"Oh God help us." Katherine said a silent prayer, and took hold of Tom's arm.

"Mr. and Mrs. Stevens," the Judge began, "I appreciate you and your family being here this morning. I know how difficult this situation is for you. You have clearly raised your family to the best of your abilities, with solid values and principals and that is a credit to you. However, it is not uncommon to find that, not withstanding the efforts of good parents, their children sometimes do not always turn out right. I am not saying that this is the case with your son. A jury will make that determination. However, in spite of the fact that your son has not had any problems with the law in the past, he does now stand before this court accused of a brutal murder. More over the evidence presented thus far by the prosecuting attorney is substantial. In cases involving lesser crimes the past record and reputation of the defendant provides the court with some indication of future behavior, and that is taken into consideration when determining if bail is appropriate. However, the reasons why people murder other people often defy logic and understanding, and therefore such behavior is seldom predictable, in light of their past actions or reputation. For this reason, I must deny bail in this case, and order that your son remain in custody pending his trial."

"Wait a minute. You can't do that. He didn't kill anyone." Tom was on his feet and moving toward the railing. Hingle turned to stop him.

"Tom, sit down. You are not helping John." He himself was stung by the Judge's action, and was at a loss for any words that could soften the blow. Katherine and Martha held each other; and Matt moved forward to help restrain his father. Two guards moved quickly to escort John from the courtroom. Another moved toward Tom. Within minutes it was over, and the family stood in disbelief at how cold and heartless the process seemed to be. Tom turned to Hingle.

"What the hell was that? That's not what you said would happen." Tom was slow to anger but there was no mistaken the rage that was building inside him.

"I know. I know. Take it easy, Tom." Hingle was still visibly shaken.

"Take it easy? Are you crazy? They just dragged my son out of here, and you want me to take it easy?"

"Look, these things sometimes happen. We will deal with it. I will move for a speedy trial and get Tom off on the merits of the case as soon as possible." Hingle was struggling to regain some composure, and to assert an appearance of confidence and control.

"Now, you listen to me, Tom took Hingle by his silk necktie. This is my son's life we are dealing with here, not some junky who you don't give a shit about. I don't want to hear your legal bullshit. If you can't handle this case, just say so. I want the best God damned defense that you are capable of, or I'll find someone else. Do you understand me?"

"Yes, yes I understand, but this is not the place for this. Can we go back to my office where we can discuss this calmly?" Hingle for the first time realized that Tom Stevens was not a man to take lightly.

CHAPTER 18

The following five months were extremely difficult for the family. Tom and Katherine made monthly visits to Angola State Prison, where John was being held. The prison had a very bad reputation, and with each visit, they could see John's fear and desperation growing. He had managed to avoid contact with several three hundred pound gorillas, each of whom wanted to marry him; but he did not know how long he could avoid a confrontation with them. There was no way he could tell his parents about these things.

As it was, Tom was being eaten alive by a sense of helplessness and frustration, and Katherine could not keep from crying all the way back to Bay St. Louis after each visit. They did everything they could to keep John's spirits up, but with each visit their own sense of desperation was beginning to take its toll. There were few nights that Katherine did not cry herself to sleep; and Tom could think of nothing but his son, and the peril that surrounded him.

And now, there was more trouble in the family. After Michael's failure to appear at the bail hearing, Martha found out that Kimberly's family had forbidden their daughter and Michael to have anything to do with the case. Martha and Michael got into a massive fight over family loyalty, which ended in Michael siding with his wife and avoiding any further contact with his own family. This added immensely to Katherine's heartache, and brought great disappointment to Tom. However, with their every thought being consumed by John's problem, they had no time to deal with Michael's defection from the family in this time of trouble.

Martha and Matt were also beginning to feel the strain. Martha could not focus on her work, and her lack of performance in the office was beginning to attract attention. Matt was as supportive as he could be, calling his folks almost every night to inquire about their well being and John's status. But, he too was being torn between the family troubles and his commitment to his company and clients.

The good news was that Hingle made good on his promise to get an early trial date. It was set for November eighth. Such an early trial, within six months of the murder, was unheard of in New Orleans. Nevertheless, six months was still a long time for John to survive in Angola. The real downside of the early trial date was that Hingle had begun to appreciate the Herculean challenge that he had before him. The evidence against John was overwhelming. During the last five months, his legal team had interviewed witnesses and poured over the crime scene evidence trying to find anything that would point away from his client. His investigators had uncovered nothing that might establish an alternate motive for Mary's murder. In fact they could find no one who could say a bad word against her.

There were John's friends who attended the party. They all wanted to help, but none of them could offer any hard evidence to refute the State's case. Worse than that, Hingle was certain that Stern would cleverly use each of these witnesses to testify about the quarrel, and strengthen his case, as to motive. Not that motive was his only strong card. Far from it. He had John at the scene, with his fingerprints all over the murder weapon. As much as he tried to resist the thought, Hingle could only conclude that John was the most probable suspect. This conclusion had been plaguing Hingle for the last two weeks, and with only eight weeks left before the trial date, he was still at a loss for an effective defense strategy.

But, how could this young man so viciously murder the girl he professed to love and wanted to marry? That question kept him awake at night. He could use the witnesses to establish the love that John and Mary had for each other. That might diminish the significance of the disagreement they had that night. After all, every couple has a fight now and then. That might take away the motive in the jurors' minds. With little or no motive, the jury would then conclude that John's murdering Mary would have been a totally irrational act. Hingle could try that argument, hoping that the jury might disregard the rest of the evidence, and conclude that someone else must have entered the apartment and killed her. He could argue that, but he had already decided that he would not. He could not convince a jury of something he, himself, did not believe.

After weeks of struggling with the facts and evidence, Hingle was now ready to build the only defense he could see. He would argue that Mary Simmon's killing was totally irrational, that she had indeed been viciously murdered by someone who was out of his mind. And, that someone was John Stevens who was so drunk, that to this day he has no recollection of the crime. That would be his defense. While John may have in fact killed Mary, his alcohol induced altered state diminished his capacity to realize what he was doing.

For the last several days, he had been putting off the inevitable. He would have to talk to John, and then he would have to face Tom Stevens with his new strategy. He did not look forward to either meeting, but time was now of the essence.

CHAPTER 19

"No. No. No. I could never ever do that." John had listened quietly for the last thirty minutes while Hingle first reviewed the evidence, and then led him through a scenario that resulted in his killing Mary, while in a drunken rage. Hingle had laid out a plausible chain of events, but John just could not accept the conclusion. "That is just absurd. I could never believe that I did that to Mary."

"John, you don't know what you did from the time you passed out on the floor until you woke up in the bath tub with the murder weapon. Now, you tell me how we can explain that." Hingle was betting that John's training would make him recognize how vulnerable he was.

"I don' know." John crossed his arms on the table and buried his face. "I don't know what happened. I don't know what I did. But, I couldn't do that."

"*You* didn't do it. *You* couldn't do it." Hingle pressed. "Not if you were in your right mind, you couldn't. But, you were not in your right mind that night. You were somebody else. Don't you see?" He gave John a moment to think about it. "Have you ever been that drunk before?"

"Hell no. I never passed out before, and I was never so drunk that I couldn't remember what I did."

"That's my point. There are four witnesses who will tell the jury how drunk you were. Alcohol is a very potent drug. It can make a person do things he would never do normally. It can make you paranoid. It can cause hallucinations; make you see things that aren't there. Maybe you didn't know it was Mary."

John's head was spinning. Did any of this make sense? The possibility that Hingle might be right meant that he was responsible for Mary's terrible death. How could he live with that? On the other hand if he did do such a horrendous act while totally drunk, was he really responsible for his actions? He also knew there was no way that he could establish his innocence. All the evidence pointed to him. Tears began to run down his face, and he was overcome by the hopelessness of the situation. He looked at Hingle.

"What do you want me to do?"

"Look, John, my job is to develop a defense that will give you your life back. Now, I know the idea that you may have killed Mary is tearing you apart, but Mary is gone. We have to focus on you now. We have to use everything we have, and I really think this is the best shot we've got." John sat up and wiped his face with his shirt.

"What will happen?"

"Okay." Hingle had anticipated this question but he wanted John to ask it. "The first thing I would do is meet with the Prosecutor. I'll tell him that you are prepared to accept responsibility for Mary's death, even though you have no recollection of the circumstances. I'll tell him that you are aware of the evidence against you, and with no other explanation, you are distraught over the possibility that you might have done it. I'll remind him that there are four witnesses that will verify how drunk you were. If he buys it, he may agree to reduce the charges to involuntary manslaughter. You may have to do two or three years."

"Two or three years? In here? I can't do that. I'll never survive."

"John, you got to think about the alternative. If you are convicted of second degree murder, you will spend the rest of your life in here."

"What if he says no?" John felt overwhelmed by the terrible choices that were being hurled at him. "What if he doesn't believe that it happened that way?"

"Well," Hingle cocked his head. "it's still our best defense. Listen to me. If he rejects the idea outright, and decides to push for second degree, he will have to make that case. That means he will have to prove that you intended to kill her. If he can't do that, the jury will have to acquit." Hingle paused to see if John was getting the picture.

"What you are saying is; I admit to killing Mary, but I say that I was too drunk to know what I was doing. And, if the jury believes that, they will not convict me of second- degree murder because there was no intent on my part. And if they don't convict on second degree as charged the law will not allow them to find me guilty of a lesser charge?"

"You got it." Hingle was quite proud of himself. But John was far less comfortable with the plan.

"Are you telling me that the only way out of this is to admit to murdering the girl I loved, which I know in my heart I couldn't do?" Hingle shook his head in agreement, but said nothing. "How can I do that? What do I say to her parents? How could I live with myself?" Hingle stood up, packed some documents into his brief case, and prepared to leave.

"I'm telling you that unless we use this alcohol thing to our advantage, we will be playing Stern's game and he will destroy us with the evidence and the fact that you and Mary had a fight the night she was killed." John leaned back in his chair, laced his fingers on top of his head, and stared at the ceiling. At a loss for words, he held his breath, and then slowly released the pressure in his lungs.

"I need to talk to my Dad about this."

"Of course you do, and so do I." Hingle was moving toward the door. "I have a meeting with him this afternoon. I want him to understand where we stand, and what our options are. He is coming to my office at three-thirty. I'll have him give you a call as soon as we finish."

"He is not going to like this." John was on his feet.

"Well you are probably right about that, but I think when he realizes the difficulty of the situation, he will appreciate this defense strategy." He shook John's hand as the guard let him out of the interview room.

CHAPTER 20

"You cannot be serious. After five months of working on this case, you want my son to plead guilty to something he didn't do. What the hell kind of a lawyer are you?" Hingle had predicted Tom's reaction.

"I didn't say that. I said if the prosecution accepted his plea to involuntary manslaughter, he would get a considerably lighter sentence; but if he chooses to plead not guilty, our best defense will be based on his diminished capacity at the time." Tom was on his feet, making Hingle feel very uncomfortable.

"But that's the same thing. Isn't it? Don't you have to establish that he killed that girl before this diminished capacity bullshit can be considered?"

"Not exactly, he can plead not guilty to second degree murder, and I will then demonstrate to the jury that in his condition he could not satisfy the intent requirement of that charge. Whether he killed her or not is not the issue. The issue is whether or not he committed second-degree murder, as defined by the law. If he did not, he will go free". Tom did not like this legal mumbo jumbo. He knew his son was not capable of killing anyone and he wanted that made clear.

"Haven't you found anything that points to John's innocence? The fact is, he did not do it. That means somebody else did. There's a God damned killer out there. Doesn't anyone care about that?"

"That may be true, but the police believe John is the killer and they are not interested in looking for another one. As far as our work goes, we have interviewed everyone, and we have been over all the evidence. We can find nothing that would suggest that somebody wanted Mary Simmons dead, and there is nothing in the apartment that supports the theory that someone else entered the apartment and killed her." Tom was pacing.

"What about somebody from the project there, St.Thomas? That place is close by. Maybe some junky broke in and robbed her and killed her. Did you consider that?"

"Tom, there was no break in. There was no robbery. She was beaten, and stabbed eighteen times. There were no fingerprints unaccounted for in the apartment, or bloody footprints leading out of the apartment, and the only fingerprints on the murder weapon are John's. A junky would have to be very angry to kill like that, and very careful not to leave any trace of evidence. More improbable, he would have to go to great lengths to wipe the knife clean and somehow get John's finger prints on it." Hingle could have won this case, hands down, for the prosecution. It was difficult for Tom to deny what he knew in his heart to be true, and to look at the evidence as a stranger would. He was glad that Katherine was not up to making this meeting. He was now beginning to understand what Hingle was trying to tell him. It made no difference whether John was guilty or innocent. The only thing that mattered was what the jury would believe. And, in light of the evidence, he had to agree that John's guilt was far more believable than his innocence. It was hard to accept that his son might spend the rest of his life in prison for a crime he did not commit, but he was well aware that there were many innocent men in prison, just as there were many O.J. Simpsons, running around free. Justice was not only blind; it could be down right stupid.

"So you are convinced that this is the only way we can keep John out of prison?" Tom was asking a question to which he already knew the answer, but he hoped that he might be wrong.

"I think so, Tom, but there is no guarantee. The prosecutor is tough. No one knows what a jury will do. That's why I want you and John to think hard about trying to cut a deal for involuntary manslaughter. Your son is expecting to hear from you."

That afternoon, Tom drove to Angola to talk with his son. As John approached the glass wall between them, Tom saw the bruise and stitches over John's left eye. He tried not to over react, as they both reached for the phone. "How are you doing, Son?"

"I'm alright, Dad." He tried to sound convincing. "Had a little beef in the mess hall with some jerk over a carton of milk."

"What happened?"

"He asked me if he could have my milk. I said no, and he hit me in the eye with a metal tray. I guess I should have given him the milk. I'm all right." Tom could do nothing but look at his son and try to overcome the feeling of helplessness that was tearing at his gut.

"Are you sure? Did you report it to anyone?"

"Dad it was nothing. It's over. The last thing you do in here is report an incident like this to anyone. I said I banged my head on my bunk. They stitched me up, and that's all anyone needs to know. How is mom doing?" Tom let it drop. He had more important things to discuss with his son.

"Your mother is okay. She's tired, not sleeping well, but she's doing all right. John, I know Hingle talked with you. He met with me also. The news is not good, is it? It seems there are no good options at this time."

"Dad, John Interrupted. I've been thinking about it. I do not want to plead guilty to something I did not do. I know Hingle wants to plea bargain, but if it means I have to say I killed Mary, I just can't do that."

"But, John, do you understand that if you plead not guilty, you could lose the case, and spend the rest of your life in here." Tom, hated to be so blunt, but the possibility was real and he and John had to make sure they both understood it.

"I know that's a possibility, but Hingle says he thinks he can establish that, because I was drunk, I could not be guilty of second degree murder."

"I understand that, but there is a chance that he will lose that argument." Tom continued to play the devil's advocate.

"I know, Dad, but even if I did kill her, which is stupid even to consider, I was so drunk that I don't remember anything. That's the truth. I think I would like to take my chances with the truth, rather than to plead guilty to something I didn't do. Besides, if I plead guilty, my law career is over before it begins. I need to be found not guilty in order to get on with my life." Tom looked at John. In his heart he agreed with his son's decision. It was the same decision he would make if the situation were reversed.

"It's a tough call, Son, but it's your life, and it's your decision. You know we'll be behind you all the way, no matter what happens. He put his palm against the window. John nodded and covered his dad's hand with his own.

"I know, Dad. I am so sorry for bringing this on you and Mom."

CHAPTER 21

The remaining weeks before the trial passed quickly. Hingle was not happy with John's decision, and wanted to know how the prosecutor would have reacted to his involuntary manslaughter idea. During a preliminary meeting to review the potential witness list, he had an opportunity to suggest that his client hypothetically might be willing to plead to the lesser charge. He was stunned by Stern's answer. Not only would he not discuss it, but he also unequivocally dismissed the idea.

"No way. Your client is guilty of murder two. That's what we are going for, and we will prove it."

The answer was so disconcerting to Hingle that he decided not to discuss it with John, and certainly not his father. After all, they had already made their decision. They did not need to know that the manslaughter plea was no longer a possible option. Besides, he had enough to do now, preparing his witnesses, and lining up experts to testify to the influences of alcohol. Certainly he would use John's friends to talk about his relationship with Mary and his general character. They, of course, would be critical in establishing John's condition on the night of the crime. He would also call on at least one of John's law professors to reinforce John's dedication and commitment while at Tulane, and to help cast John as the *All American Boy*.

He wrestled with the idea of putting John on the stand, and was leaning toward doing it. John was intelligent. He was convincing, and
Hingle felt that he could win the sympathy of the jury. Actually, there
was not much that John could say under cross-examination that could
hurt him. If John was telling the truth, he had no idea who killed Mary,
or what happened. That's all he could say, if he was telling the truth.
That was the one reservation that Hingle had. If John were lying, putting him on the stand would be a fatal error. Stern would get to the
truth eventually. If John was not absolutely truthful, Stern would trip
him up, and it would be all over. He discussed the matter with John and
Tom, and after considering the pros and cons, they agreed that the jury
would want to hear John's story directly from him. He would testify.

The media loved the story. In a city where blacks were killing blacks
everyday over drugs, this trial had real sex appeal. There was the beautiful young white victim, a brilliant student, and promising lawyer. There
was the defendant, her lover, also a budding lawyer, and also white. The
crime itself was extraordinary in its brutality. The trial promised to be
front-page news to the end.

On Monday morning, November 8, 1998 Judge Patrick Quinton's
courtroom was packed. As expected, the press was well represented.
Among the crowd of onlookers sat four very somber parents. Behind
the defense table, Tom and Katherine held on to each other, filled with
apprehension for their son. Across the aisle were two other dedicated
parents, still heartbroken over their loss. Bob and Margaret Simmons
wanted to find some understanding of what happened to their daughter. They needed desperately to find some way to close this terrible
experience.

"All rise, the Third District Court of the City of New Orleans is in
session, Judge Patrick Quinton presiding." The bailiff brought the
courtroom to order. "Be seated." The judge looked over the sea of faces

in his courtroom, being reminded of the crowds that must have gathered at the Coliseum thousands of years earlier. Quinton was highly respected as a no-nonsense, tough but fair judge. His balding head and gray beard were symbolic of the wisdom that he had gained during his sixty-five years. He dispatched the preliminaries with little ceremony and directed the Prosecutor to make his opening statement. Stern's serious demeanor foretold his thorough and surgically concise presentation of the elements of his case. Means, motive and opportunity, it was a textbook presentation. He walked the jury through each point, leaving little doubt that he would give them what they needed to convict the defendant beyond a reasonable doubt. In closing he approached the jury box, and lowered his voice as if to share a secret with them.

"This was not a typical crime of passion, ladies and gentlemen. This was brutally executed. Miss Simmons was beaten, and then stabbed eighteen times. When you listen to Mr. Hingle tell you about this wonderful young man who he represents, I would ask that you remember that fact - eighteen times." He did not thank them, but walked quietly back to his seat leaving them to ponder the gruesome picture in their minds.

"Mr. Hingle" The Judge turned towards the defense table.

"Thank you, Your Honor." Hingle, himself, was having difficulty erasing Stern's well-rendered image from his mind. He took his time approaching the jury box, and paused long enough to allow the members to refocus their attention on him. "**Quid Pro Quo**, Ladies and Gentlemen, the Latin phrase literally means 'this for that'. Something is given in exchange for something received. Some action is taken in response to something done. When we are victims of an injustice, it is our nature to want to strike back. When someone hurts us, we want to return the hurt. There is a human need in each of us that wants to get even. '**Quid Pro Quo**'. That impulse is stronger in some of us than in others; and sometimes, when revenge is taken, the '**quo**' does not always equal the 'quid'. Often the response is emotionally charged and excessive; and typically the consequences are tragic for all concerned." Hingle wanted that idea to penetrate. He tried to make eye contact with several of the jurors. "Horrible crimes committed in our society also demand punishment. There must be a 'Quid Pro Quo' extracted before good citizens can rest easily. But, ours is a civilized society, a society of laws. Specific penalties for crimes committed against us are prescribed by those laws; and those penalties are not subject to emotional interpretation. As jurors, you have an awesome responsibility to set aside your own emotions in determining whether the prescribed penalty should be inflicted upon a defendant. Your job is to determine if the defendant has indeed committed a specific crime and therefore must pay the penalty for it. In carrying out that responsibility, each of you has a solemn obligation to consider all the facts, and to weigh all the evidence, so that, with the help of God, the punishment that you do impose is warranted; and the 'Quid Pro Quo' that you extract is fare and just."

Hingle pointed toward his client. "Mr. Stern is right about one thing, ladies and gentlemen. I am going to tell you that John Steven's is a fine young man, from a strong God-fearing family. Just like any of your families. Just like any of your sons. You will come to know him better through this trial. You will learn about his reputation. You will appreciate his hard work as a student, and his dedication in graduating from Tulane University Law School. You will hear from his friends, and law professors who knew him well. You will hear about the great love that he had for Miss Mary Simmons. And, when you have reviewed the events of that evening," He paused. "that evening which started out so wonderfully and ended so tragically - when you have had the opportunity to learn the facts, and understand the evidence, ladies and gentlemen, there will be no doubt in your minds that this young man could not be responsible for the terrible murder for which he stands accused. And, he should not be punished for it. Yes, this terrible crime cries out for a "Quid Pro Quo", but condemning this young man to spend the rest of his life in prison for it would be wrong, and a terrible injustice. Thank you."

Katherine liked hearing good things about her son. It was what she wanted the world to know about him. Tom thought there would be more.

Stern wasted no time calling his first witness, the criminal pathologist who conducted the autopsy. "Your Honor, the people call to the stand Doctor René La Chappell." The doctor was as round as he was tall, but his comical stature did not detract from his expertise. His testimony was graphic. Stern led him to elaborate on the type of wounds and the angle of entry. How many times was she stabbed? Where was she stabbed? Were there defensive wounds? He asked about the type of weapon that could have been used, and he established that the recovered knife was the probable weapon. He talked in great detail about the blood found at the scene. Then came the pictures. Disturbingly graphic photographs of the body, taken at sensational angles, Stern entered them into evidence, and passed them to the jury. He continued to ring every last drop of testimony from the doctor. Hingle objected to nothing. When Stern had finally exhausted the witness, he turned him over. "Your witness." Hingle looked at the pictures, now before him on the table.

"Doctor, what do these pictures and your examination of the body tell you about this crime and the perpetrator?"

"This was a very frenetic attack." The doctor responded quickly. "The attacker slashed wildly at the victim, almost out of control. The damage done to the body far exceeded what was needed to kill her. The killer was obviously in a highly agitated state of mind to inflict this damage."

"Highly agitated." Hingle picked up on the last statement. Does that mean abnormal?"

"Yes" abnormal, irrational. I suppose you could say that."

"No more questions at this time, Your Honor. Defense reserves the right to recall this witness."

"The witness is excused. Ladies, and Gentlemen," Judge Quinton addressed the jury. "it is close to the lunch hour, and I think this is probably a good time to take a break. We will reconvene at two o'clock.

CHAPTER 22

The bailiff recalled the courtroom to order at exactly two o'clock and the Judge wasted no time getting started.

"Your next witness, Mr. Stern"

"People call Sergeant Benjamin Bell, Your Honor"

Sergeant Bell looked bigger and more impressive in his dress uniform. Stern identified Bell for the record; and established that he was the first officer at the scene of the crime.

"Can you describe for us what you found when you arrived at the apartment, Sergeant." Bell lumbered through his testimony, describing the scene in great detail.

"And then I seen Mr. Stevens there."

"Will you point out the person you identified as Mr. Stevens, Sergeant?" Sterns interrupted. "Is he in the courtroom?"

"Yes, sir, he is sitting right over there." Bell pointed at John.

"Let the record show that Sergeant Bell has identified the defendant." Stern's dialogue was abrupt, almost mechanical. "Was there anyone else in the apartment when you arrived?"

"No, Sir, just Mr. Stevens."

"What did Mr. Stevens have to say, Sergeant?"

"Well, he was pretty messed-up. Didn't really seem to know what was going on. He told me, he woke up in the bathtub; and then he found the victim in the kitchen. Then, he returned to the bathroom and found the weapon; and then he called 911."

"Did you see the weapon?"

"Yes, Sir. Mr. Stevens took me into the bathroom, and showed me the knife in the bathtub." Stern walked to the evidence table and returned with a long carving knife sealed in a plastic bag. He handed him the knife that had been taken from the scene.

"Is this the knife you saw?" Bell examined the weapon.

"Yes, Sir, that's certainly looks like it." Stern passed the knife by Hingle and displayed it to the jury.

"Ask that this weapon be entered into evidence as peoples' exhibit 001. What did you do when the defendant showed you the knife?"

"Well, Sir, I sealed off the bathroom and waited for the detectives to arrive. They came and took some pictures and then bagged the knife for evidence." Stern approached the witness.

"Did the defendant touch that knife at any time while you were in the apartment?"

"No, Sir. No, Sir, he did not."

"Thank you Sergeant. Your witness." Hingle stood up.

"Good afternoon, Sergeant Bell. You stated that the defendant didn't real seem to know what was going on. What did you mean by that?"

"Well, Sir he was like in a fog. He didn't seem to be able to concentrate on what I was asking him. He didn't seem to be able to focus on what was happening."

"And when he took you into the bathroom to see the knife, what was the condition of the bathroom". Bell looked puzzled.

"The condition of the bathroom, Sir?"

"Yes, was it neat, clean?"

"Oh no, Sir, Mr. Stevens, he got sick in there and it was a mess, all over the floor. Smelled pretty bad too." Hingle walked away from the witness, toward the defense table.

"So, Mr. Stevens had vomited on the bathroom floor; and as you said he was acting like he was in a fog;" Hingle checked his notes. "didn't seem to be able to concentrate; didn't seem to know what was going on; couldn't focus. Isn't that right? Is that what you said?"

"Yes, Sir."

"Let me ask you something, Sergeant Bell. Have you ever had a real bad hang over, after a night of heavy drinking?" Hingle sat down, not expecting to get an answer. He was right.

"Objection, Your Honor, irrelevant." Stern was on his feet.

"Sustained."

"I withdraw the question, Your Honor. Hingle half stood, and quickly sat down. "No more questions." Stern then called a police forensic expert to verify that the fingerprints on the knife belonged to John, and to establish that the chain of evidence had not been broken. The witness had just begun what promised to be lengthy testimony describing how he found not only a full set of finger prints on the knife but also a full palm print belonging to John, when Hingle suddenly dropped a bomb.

"Your honor, the defense will stipulate that the finger prints on the knife belong to my client, Mr. Stevens." The concession stopped Stern cold. Placing the defendant's prints on the knife was a major element of his case. While the evidence was irrefutable, he did not expect such a gift from the defense counsel.

"In that case, Your Honor, the people have no further questions. Your witness, Mr. Hingle." Hingle approached the witness stand.

"Lieutenant Clinton, is it?"

"Yes."

"Do you have any idea how those prints got on that knife?"

"Objection, Your Honor." Stern was up. "Calls for speculation. The witness can only verify that the prints are those of the defendant. He can not testify as to how they came to be on the weapon."

"I'm asking the witness if he knows." Hingle responded.

"Over ruled. Answer the question, if you know." The witness turned from the Judge to Hingle.

"No, Sir. I can't say exactly how they got there, I can only assume..."

"Thank you, Mr. Clinton." Hingle cut him off. "No more questions, at this time." Stern had expected the forensic testimony to last the entire afternoon, and he was somewhat taken back, by Hingle's tactics. He needed a few minutes to rethink his approach.

"Your, Honor, the prosecution asks for a brief recess at this time."

"Mr. Stern, it is now three-thirty. How much time do you need?" Judge Quinton was not comfortable with the motion.

"About a half hour, Your Honor."

"That would bring us to four o'clock which is late in the day to begin new testimony. I'm going to deny that request and ask you to call your next witness now." Stern's strategy was to devote at least a day to establish motive. He had planned to parade each of the four friends, who had attended the party, before the jury. His questioning would be pointed, using each witness to confirm the prior friend's testimony and build on it. Now, he would not be able to do that within the time left before the day's adjournment. He decided to change tack and call his strongest witness first.

"Call Karen Burns." John turned to watch as Karen passed the railing and approached witness stand. She smiled at him before raising her right hand, swearing to tell the truth. She tried to make herself comfortable in the oversize mahogany witness chair.

"Good afternoon, Miss Burns." Stern asked her to identify herself for the record, and tell the jury how she had come to know the defendant. Karen talked about being introduced to John through Allison Mc Kay. Suddenly, the mention of her friend's name brought tears to Karen's eyes.

"I'm sorry."

"Are you okay, Miss Burns?" Stern anticipated that the tragic deaths of the two other classmates would come up during the trial. The murder of Mary Stevens was difficult enough, but the senseless hit and run deaths of two more Tulane students within twenty-four hours was devastating to everyone who knew the three girls. He decided to let Karen have as much time as she needed to talk about the accident, and to regain her composure. He did not want the hit and run to become the focal point of the trial and distract the jury from his case. It would be better to deal with it early and let it pass.

"Yes, I'm alright." She wiped her eyes with a tissue. "Allison, and Courtney Roberts were killed in a car crash, right after Mary was killed. No one could believe it. We were all trying to deal with Mary's death when we heard the news about the accident. It was terrible." Karen rambled on about her friends, how they met, and the fun they had together. "They did not deserve to die like that. Nobody can understand why it happened. Allison and I were very close. I miss her a lot."

"I'm sure you do, Miss Burns." Now, Stern had a problem. His line of questioning for Karen would not be easy on her. In fact, he intended to manipulate her, and extract some testimony that would be damaging to the defendant. He needed to be tough with her but he did not want to appear heartless to the members of the jury. Since Karen now had their total sympathy for the loss of her three friends, he decided to give the jury something else to consider about Karen Burns. This would allow him to stall for time, and save her important testimony for the next day. "Karen, do you know Martin Feeny?"

"Yes." Karen had not expected the question.

"How well do you know, Mr. Feeny?"

"He's a friend. I met him at school. He just graduated with John and the others from Law School."

"Isn't it true that he is a little more than a friend? Isn't it true that you and Mr. Feeny are living together."

"Objection, Your Honor." Hingle did not like these questions. "The witness' relationship with Mr. Feeny is not relevant to this case."

"I'm inclined to agree, Mr. Stern. Where are you going with this?" Judge Quinton asked.

"Your, Honor, both Miss Burns and Mr. Feeny are key witnesses in this case. The relationship that they share is relevant to the testimony that they may give about each other." Stern was actually less concerned about the relationship than he was about the time. If he could keep this line of questioning going for another twenty minutes, Quinton might recess until the morning. The judge raised his eyes to the ceiling, considering Stern's answer.

"I'll allow the question. Objection overruled."

"Isn't that true Miss Burns?"

"Isn't what true?"

"That you and Mr. Feeny are living together and you share an intimate relationship with him." Stern took the opportunity to rephrase the question.

"Yes we live together."

"And you're sleeping with him?" Karen was annoyed by this intrusion into her private life, and her Irish temper was beginning to show. "Yes, I am sleeping with him. Is that a crime?"

"No, it's not a crime. How long have you known Mr. Feeny?"

"Your Honor" Hingle had had enough. "Objection."

"Sustained." Quinton was becoming impatient. "I think you have established the relationship between the witness and Mr. Feeny. Will counsels approach the bench?" Quinton leaned forward as Hingle and Stern huddled in front of him. "How much more do you have for this witness, Mr. Stern?"

"Actually, quite a bit, Your Honor." Stern was anticipating the Judge's impatience. "I intend to question her in detail about the events leading to the murder."

"Okay then, I think we'll call it for today." He dismissed the attorneys and addressed the jury. "Ladies and Gentlemen, It's after four, and I know you have a long day ahead of you, tomorrow. I'm going to adjourn for today, and remind you that you are not to discuss the case with anyone. Thank you."

CHAPTER 23

Neither Martha nor Matt attended the first day of trial. Martha had spoken with her parents earlier in the week and explained that she was having trouble at work. She did not want them to think that she wasn't concerned about John or them, but her supervisor had warned her about her work. In the past few weeks since the murder, she'd had trouble concentrating, and was responsible for some serious mistakes. Now, she was on notice. She promised to fly to New Orleans as soon as she could put a holiday weekend together, but it was not a good idea to ask for more time off, right now.

Matt was very candid with his folks. He would lend as much support as possible to them and John, but he needed to do it very quietly. The advertising business was extremely sensitive to public opinion. Clients were very squeamish about having their products connected in anyway to unpleasant news events. The reputation of their account executive was important to them, and even though John had not been convicted of anything, Matt had been advised by the company executives to keep a very low profile regarding his brother's situation. They agreed that Matt should periodically take a day off under some pretense to visit with his family in New Orleans, but the less said about the situation the better. He would fly to New Orleans on Friday.

Katherine and Tom would have felt better to have their family close by at a time like this, but they understood that Martha, Matt and Michael all had their own lives to live. Certainly, they could not be expected to put their responsibilities on hold until John's problems were resolved. Still, Tom could not but feel a sense of disappointment. He had expected John's brothers and sister to rally around him in his time of trouble; at least he hoped they would. It was easy to remain close and supportive in good times, but a family's metal can only be tested when it suffers the stress and hardship of the bad times. This was the first real test for his family. Tom prayed they would all survive, and be together at the end of the ordeal.

In a way, not having the others to be concerned about enabled Tom to concentrate more on John and Katherine. Katherine, in particular, was not holding up well. Being so close to John in the courtroom, but unable to comfort him, gave her great distress. She was becoming withdrawn and despondent. He felt a little better about John. Not that he underestimated the serious trouble that his son was in; but he was confident of his innocence, and both he and John believed in the legal system. It was important to remain strong and positive for John's sake. That was the most important thing in his life now.

He and Katherine had decided to drive to the trial early each day and return to Bay St. Louis in the evening. The travel would be hard on them, and after the first day Katherine went to bed, as soon as they arrived home. He knew that it would be impossible to go through this trial and continue his own job. Fortunately, his company had been very understanding in granting him a month's leave of absence

That evening, as Tom sat, in his darkened den, alone with his thoughts, he recalled earlier days when his family was young and happy. How many times had he talked about taking a month off, just to enjoy them, but never did? As he fell asleep in his chair, mentally and physically exhausted, he now wished he had.

CHAPTER 24

The following morning, the proceedings began at 10 o'clock. Stern felt pretty good about how Monday had concluded, but now he needed to get back to his plan of action. Karen Burns had already been sworn, and she seemed a little more intense than the day before. She was ready to do battle with Stern over her relationship with Martin Feeny, but Stern was no longer interested Martin Feeny.

"Good Morning Miss Burns"

"Good Morning."

"Miss Burns, I'd like to talk to you about the events of Sunday evening May 7, 1998. That was the day you graduated from Tulane. Do you recall?"

"Do I recall that I graduated from Tulane?" Karen said sarcastically. She wanted Stern to know that she was still upset from the day before, and she was not going to let him push her around.

"No, Miss Burns," Stern turn toward her and smiled. "I'm interested in what happened that evening. You had dinner with some friends that night. Isn't that true?"

"Yes, that's true."

"Well, tell us about that. Who were you with? Where did you have dinner? What did you do after dinner?" Stern needed to loosen her up. She was much too defensive for his purposes. Karen had been through this before with the police, and she did not want to say anything that could be misconstrued. She recounted everything that happened precisely up to the group's arrival at John's apartment. "Now when you were at Mr. Steven's apartment did something happen that caused the mood of the party to change?" Stern began to focus.

"If you mean the fight, yes, it happened," Karen was anxious to set the record straight "but it was nothing like what was reported on TV." Stern didn't expect the fastball right down the middle, but he hit it out of the park.

"The fight? What fight was that?"

"It was over nothing. John and I knew each other before he met Mary, and when we were kissing goodbye on the couch; we kind of forgot where we were. Mary got upset and threw a glass of water at us. So, Feeny and I left, and that was the end of it." This was getting better than he could have hoped for. Stern was not aware of this prior relationship and jumped at the opportunity to pursue it.

"How well did you and Mr. Stevens know each other?"

"We dated for a while. John is a real nice guy. I liked him a lot, but then he met Mary, and I was history." That was all Karen wanted to say about that, but Stern pressed on.

"Did you know Mr. Stevens as well as you know Martin Feeny?"

"Objection, Your Honor." Hingle could not afford to have this witness further discredited.

"No, I'll allow it. You can answer the question, Miss Burns."

"What exactly are you asking me?" Karen resisted.

"I'm asking you if you had an intimate relationship with John Stevens." Stern turned and approached her. " Did you have a sexual relationship with him." Karen looked at John and hesitated before answering.

"Yes, but only for a short time."

"And, was Mary Simmons aware of that brief sexual relationship."

"No, not at first, but I think she suspected it later on."

"And why do you think that?" Stern dug a little deeper hoping to strike gold.

"Well, John continued to treat me nicely after we broke up, and I think she suspected we had been more than friends."

"I see. So you and John still had a thing for each other?"

"No, not exactly, but we remained good friends."

"Okay, now, Miss Burns, I have one more question." Stern was now facing the jury. "What did John Stevens say when Mary threw the water at him and you?"

Karen shifted uncomfortably in her chair. "Well, he was pretty upset. He called her a bitch, but he didn't mean it." Stern continued to look at the jury.

"He called her a bitch. Did he ever call you a bitch?"

"No"

"Thank you Miss Burns. I have no further questions." This was not good. Hingle knew he had to do some fast damage control as he approached the witness.

"Miss Burns, John Stevens was not having a romantic relationship with you while he was seeing Miss Simmons, was he?"

"No, he was not."

"How would you describe his relationship with Miss Simmons?"

"They were very close. I think they were in love."

"Thank you, Miss Burns. Your Honor, I have no more questions of Miss Burns at this time, however we reserve the right to call her as a defense witness." Stern smiled again at Karen as she passed by.

CHAPTER 25

"The people call Mr. David Churchill." Churchill raised his hand as the Bailiff did his job.

"Do you swear to tell the truth, the whole truth, and nothing but the truth, so help you God?"

"I will. I mean I do." Churchill was very nervous about his testimony. When the police finally questioned him several days after the murder, he told them that he left the party early and knew nothing that could help them with the murder.

"Good morning Mr. Churchill." Stern did not wait for Churchill to return the greeting. "I wonder if you would recall for us the events that took place on the night of May 7, 1998."

"Well, we met at the Café Giovanni for dinner." Churchill had been over and over his testimony in his own mind, determined not to say anything that would be incriminating. He spoke very cautiously, and Stern let him go, asking questions intermittently, until the witness appeared to be more relaxed. Stern then directed his attention to the scene of the murder.

"Did you attend a party on that evening in the apartment of the defendant."

"Yes, I did. Well, it wasn't really a party. We just went back there after we had dinner to hang out and have a few beers."

"Was there a time during the evening when the defendant and Miss Simmons had a quarrel."

"Yes, John and Marty Feeny were fooling around with some of the girls and Mary got mad and threw a drink at John and Karen. But, that was all. Everybody was kind a drunk. The whole thing was pretty dumb. Pat Healy and I left, right after that happened." Churchill shifted his weight.

"Did you say Miss Simmons threw a drink at Mr. Stevens and Miss Burns?"

"Yes, that's right."

"What happened after that?"

"Well, John and Karen jumped up off the couch when they got wet; and John called Mary a bitch. Then Karen grabbed Feeny and stormed out of the apartment. That's when Healy and I left." Churchill wanted to say as little as possible, but Stern wanted more.

"What was Mr. Stevens and Miss Burns doing on the couch before Miss Simmons threw the water?"

"Healy and I were watching TV in the living room, so I didn't see everything; but when I looked toward the kitchen, I saw John laying on top of Karen. It looked like they were kissing." Healy glanced toward John apologetically, realizing he was not helping him.

"So, Mr. Stevens and Karen Burns were making out on the couch, and, when Mary Simmons saw them, she threw a drink at them; at which time Stevens and Burns jumped up. Then Stevens called Miss Simmons a bitch and Miss Burns left the apartment." Stern was thinking that this was too good to be true, when Hingle finally realized what Stern was doing.

"Objection, Your Honor, the Prosecution is testifying on behalf of the witness."

"The objection is sustained. You know better than that, Mr. Stern. The jury is instructed to disregard the last statement made by the Prosecution." Stern was happy to take the reprimand. There was no way the jury could disregard the statement that Hingle let him slip in.

"No more questions, Your Honor." Hingle looked at John for some kind of explanation. John leaned toward him and whispered in his ear.

"It wasn't like it sounds. I told you Courtney pushed me. I fell over the couch and landed on top of Karen, and I kissed her. It was all over very fast." Hingle approached the witness stand.

"Mr. Churchill, how well did you known Miss Simmons and Mr. Stevens?"

"I knew them pretty well. I still consider John to be a good friend. And Mary; she was just a terrific girl. I liked her a lot."

"And how did they feel about each other?"

"Objection." Stern was on his feet. The witness cannot know how these people felt about each other." Judge Quinton sustained the objection, and Hingle was embarrassed for asking the question in that way.

"Let me rephrase that. Based on your observations, when you were with them, how do you think they felt toward each other?"

"Well, obviously, I wasn't with them all the time, but it was easy to see that they liked each other quite a bit" That was not the answer that Hingle wanted. He needed to establish their love for each other. He tried again.

"At anytime did you see them fight or have a disagreement?"

"No, I can't say that I did, except for that night."

"Okay," Hingle approached him. "Let's talk about that night. You testified that you saw John Stevens lying on top of Karen Burns. Isn't it true that he was pushed and he landed on top of her after falling over the couch?"

"Pushed?" Churchill looked puzzled. "Pushed by who?" Again, not wanting to point a finger at anyone, he answered nervously. "I told you, when I looked over at them he was already on top of Karen. I don't really know how he got there." Thinking this guy was a loose cannon, Hingle hesitated to let him say anything else, but he could not let the testimony stand.

"So you are not saying he wasn't pushed, only that you didn't see him get pushed, is that right?"

"Yes that's right."

"The defense has no more questions of the witness at this time, however we do reserve the right to recall." Hingle wondered how much more damage Churchill could do as a defense witness. He was relieved when Judge Quinton called a lunch break.

CHAPTER 26

Over lunch, Tom and Katherine discussed the proceedings, which they were finding all very disturbing. Why was Hingle not helping John? They could not understand why he was letting Stern's witnesses go unchallenged. Why was he not questioning the evidence? And why, in God's name, did he give up on the fingerprints so easily? When was he going to start talking about John's condition on the night of the crime?

They, of course, were not fully aware of Hingles strategy, which was to allow the prosecutor to establish his case with as little testimony and elaboration as possible. An extensive cross-examination of the witnesses and prolonged discussions about the evidence would only serve to give the jury more graphic details to think about. Hingle wanted the prosecution to rest, so that he could begin his defense. On direct examination he would use the witnesses as he needed. After lunch, Stern pressed on.

"Prosecution calls Mr. Martin Feeny" Martin Feeny had been waiting for his opportunity to set the record straight. John was a good friend and he was not about to let him get convicted of a crime that Feeny knew he could not commit. He was ready and anxious to help his friend. Stern approached the witness stand as Feeny was being sworn, and wasted no time with a greeting. Mr. Feeny you were in John Steven's apartment the night Mary Simmons was killed, were you not?"

"Yes I was."

"And you were a part of an altercation that happened that evening, weren't you?"

"I guess you could say that, but it wasn't anything. A little fight, that's all. Nothing happened that would cause John to kill Mary. That's for damn sure."

"Well, maybe you could tell us what caused that little fight."

"Okay. We were all drinking, right? But, John and I had a little more than the rest, because I had this pint of Jack Daniels, right? And, John and I were doing shots as we walked around the quarter, and rode the streetcar back to the apartment. So, when we get back to the apartment we're feeling really good. Actually, kind a silly." Feeny kept glancing nervously at John, looking for some kind of acquiescence and approval. "Anyway, we started telling the girls how much we were going to miss them and everything, and John starts fooling around on the couch with Karen, who's really my girl. I knew they were just kidding around because they used to go out together. But, I figure if John's with my girl, I should go after his girl, right? So, I approach Mary who was standing at the kitchen sink. But, Mary's not interested, and she starts pushing me away, and I trip over the table. Next thing I know Mary's throwing water at us. She hits Karen and John on the couch with a pan full of water, and they both jump up. Now, Karen gets really pissed off at Mary for getting her dress wet, and she grabs me, and we leave, and that was about it. That's all that happened." Stern approached.

"What did Mr. Stevens say and do when he was hit with the pan of water?"

"Well, like I said, he and Karen were really surprised by the water, and they both jumped up. I think John called Mary a bitch or something, but he didn't mean anything by it. He just had a little too much to drink; that's all. Mary had never done anything like that before, and he was really embarrassed. You know in front of Karen and the other guys, he just got really mad; is all."

"Had you ever seen him that mad before?"

"John? No, never. Not at Mary. I've seen him really pissed at me and maybe the other guys. He's got a hell of a temper, but he would never take it out on Mary."

"Well is it possible that with everything he had to drink he just lost it." Stern knew enough not to ask a question that he did not know the answer to, and this was an important question concerning motive; but he was certain that this witness, so anxious to help this friend, would give him the answer he expected.

"No way. He wasn't that drunk. Are you kidding? I had as much to drink as he did, and I was fine. As a matter of fact, I've never seen John really smashed, and we've done a lot of drinking together."

"Jesus Christ." Hingle said under his breath. He could not believe what he was hearing. This was turning into a nightmare.

"Thank you Mr. Feeny, no more questions." Stern liked the way the pieces were falling into place. Hingle could not risk any more testimony from Feeny at this time. He would wait until he had a chance to extract his story the way he wanted it during the defense. Coming as no surprise to Hingle now, Stern called the last witness who attended the party at John's apartment, Patrick Healy. As he expected, Stern was carefully milking testimony from each of the witness to establish a motive for the murder. Unfortunately, he was doing a pretty good job. "Mr. Healy, you know the defendant, John Stevens?"

"Yes, he's a friend of mine."

"And Mary Simmons, you knew her, as well?"

"Yes."

"Tell us how you know them, or knew them." The witness talked about how he had met John in their first year, and hung out together through law school. They'd become good friends, but then John met Mary and had less time for hanging out. He liked Mary, though and they always had a good time when they were together. "How often did they fight?" Stern caught Healy off guard.

"How often did they fight? I don't know. I never saw them fight." Finally, Hingle thought, this might be the testimony he had hoped for, but his enthusiasm was quickly dampened. Healy continued. "Except for that one time, on graduation night, but I think she was really out of line. She got John really upset that night."

"What exactly happened?" Stern was loving this.

"Well, I was in the living room with Churchill and apparently, Mary said something to John, or John said something to Mary, and the next thing I know there's a big fight going on between Feeny, John, Karen, Mary, and Courtney Roberts. She was one of the girls who were killed in the automobile accident. Next thing I know, Mary shoves Feeny and dumps water all over John and Karen."

"And what happened after that?"

"Well, Karen and Feeny got mad and left, and John called Mary a bitch. Churchill and I figured the party was over at that point, so we left, and went to Cooter Browns."

"Do you know what started the fight?"

"Not exactly. Everybody was having a good time and then all of a sudden all hell broke lose."

"And you and Mr. Churchill left."

"Oh yeah. We didn't want to get in the middle of that mess."

"Thank you Mr. Healy. No further questions. Your witness" Hingle stood up.

"Your honor, we have no questions at this time, but we would reserve the right to recall." He could now sense the uneasiness behind him. He glanced at Tom Stevens and could read the frustration on his face. He hoped the prosecution case would soon conclude so that he could begin his defense. But, he was disheartened by the negative testimony so far. He realized that he had his work cut out for him, and was relieved when Stern stood again.

"Your Honor, the People rest."

CHAPTER 27

Judge Quinton adjourned for the day after the prosecution rested its case. Tom could not wait to corner Hingle outside the courtroom. He and Katherine sat through the prosecution's entire case struggling to understand Hingle's reasoning; and now he wanted some answers.

"Look Mr. Hingle I'm sure you know what you're doing but I'll be damned if I do. You're going to have to explain some things to us, so that we know what's going on."

The last thing Hingle wanted to do, after a long day in court, was to explain legal procedure to Tom and Katherine. However, he knew that they were confused and before starting the defense he wanted to put their minds at ease.

"Tell you what folks, if you give me a few minutes to take care of some business and freshen up, I'd like to take you to dinner. That will give us an opportunity to catch up; and I can give you an idea of how I plan to proceed from here. It's been a long day and I think we could all use a drink and a good meal. What do you say?" Tom had a million questions, and he was more interested in some straight answers than having dinner with Hingle, but it had been a stressful day. He was hungry and he knew Katherine could use a good New Orleans's meal. A double Glenlevit on the rocks sounded pretty good to. "Okay, we can do that. Where would you like to go?"

"It's a little after five." Hingle checked his Rolex. "I need to run back to my office for a few minutes. Take me about a half hour. Why don't we plan on meeting at Emeril's at about six? I'll have my girl call ahead. How does that sound?" Tom agreed and he and Katherine left the courthouse and started up Tulane Avenue toward the small parking lot where they had left their car. As they walked along they did not hear the footsteps following them.

"Mr. Stevens" A strong male voice called out from behind him. "Can you give us a minute?" Tom and Katherine turned at the same time and immediately recognized the middle-aged couple that had been sitting across the isle from them all week in the courtroom. Tom was stunned not knowing what to expect from this encounter.

"Yes, yes, of course, Mr. Simmons. Whatever we can do." He knew that this was a difficult situation, and one that could be potentially dangerous depending on the grieving father's state of mind. He was concerned for Katherine, but that fear dissipated when he saw Mrs. Simmons holding tightly on to her husband's arm. Tom and Katherine approached the couple.

"Mr. Simmons, I don't know what I can say to you that could possible ease the pain that you both must be feeling." Tom was struggling for the correct words. "We had the pleasure of meeting your daughter. She was a beautiful girl. My son was very much in love with her, and I want you to believe that he did not do this terrible thing."

"Mr. Stevens, Mrs. Stevens," Bob Simmons responded in a calm, but saddened voice. "We don't know what to believe. "None of this makes any sense to us, but you seem to be good people, and we know this is a terrible ordeal for you, as well. Mary had written us about your son. She was anxious for us to meet him. Now, we have lost our daughter and you may lose your son. We want you to know that we take no comfort in that. We are trying very hard to find some meaning in this, so that we can let her go." Both women were now in tears. "We hope for your sake that your son is innocent; and if he is, whoever murdered our daughter is caught and punished. Margaret and I just wanted to tell you that." The two women looked at each other with deep empathy for the pain they were both feeling. Then, instinctively, Katherine stepped forward, and put her arms around Margaret. The women embraced each other, drawing from that deep well of emotion that only mothers seem to share.

"Thank you for telling us that." Katherine said. " We are so sorry."

"I know you are. May God help us all through this." Margaret said wiping her tears. Bob again took his wife's arm and they walked back toward the courthouse. Tom and Katherine watched them for a while and then walked silently to their car. They were greatly relieved in knowing that the Simmons's did not hate them or their son, but neither felt much like eating when they arrived at Emeril's.

The restaurant had been one of New Orleans finest new dining establishments, but lately the charismatic owner was spending more time cooking on talk shows than in the restaurant. Both the fare and service were suffering from it. A hostess met them at the door and showed them to Hingle's table. Within minutes, he joined them. The Stevens ordered light, while Hingle started with a cup of gumbo followed by the roast rack of lamb. He ordered a bottle of Rosemont Estate Chardonnay, 1998. They talked while they ate.

"I know you have a lot of questions." Hingle took control. "That's understandable. No one really knows how a trial will progress, especially the defense team. Sure, we know what the evidence is going in, and the witnesses are all identified, but we don't know how the Prosecution will present that evidence or how he will call the witnesses.

And, we certainly don't know what they will say. That's the problem we had this week." He adjusted the napkin hanging from his neck and took another spoonful of gumbo.

"But you didn't ask any questions. It seemed like you were letting Stern have his way without any objections from you." Tom ignored the Caesar Salad in front of him.

"That's not exactly true." Hingle washed the gumbo down with the wine. "I love this wine, Australian, not expensive. Don't forget what our strategy is. We are going to convince the jury that he is not guilty of second degree murder as defined by the law."

"But, he's not guilty at all." Katherine was listening intently, as she rearranged her salad. "Someone else killed that girl. Shouldn't you be challenging any evidence that incriminates John? Like the fingerprints; why did you drop that? If John didn't kill her, those can't be his fingerprints?"

"But they are his prints, Mrs. Stevens." Hingle wiped some blue cheese dressing from the corner of his mouth. "Look, you don't understand. The evidence is not important. We are not arguing that John did not commit the murder. Our position is; if he did, he did not do it with intent. That's the key to our defense."

"But what about all those witnesses?" Tom interrupted him. "I thought you were going to use them to establish that John was too drunk to know what he was doing? Why didn't you do that?"

"I will do that when I recall them all during the defense argument." He examined the lamb that the waiter placed before him. "But, I do have to admit, I was very disappointed with what they've said so far. None of their testimonies correlate exactly. One of them has Mary throwing a glass of water at John. Another says she threw a drink at John and Karen; and this guy Feeny says she threw a pan of water at all of them. That bothers me."

"Why does that bother you?" Tom said nervously. "Did they say anything that hurt John?"

"Not really, but they didn't exactly help him either. That's why I did not prolong their testimony. I want to start fresh with them, and direct the questioning toward the points that we need to make. I also want the jury to forget some of the things they already said."

"What things?" Katherine now was tasting the two shrimp on a lettuce leaf that Emeril offered as an entrée for $28.95."

"Well, all this talk about John and Karen on the couch is not giving the jury a good feeling. I need to turn that around. And, of course, Stern has used every one of them to establish that there was an argument and a motive. I expected that, but I did not expect to hear what I did. This last guy, Healy has a God damn brawl going on in the apartment."

"So what? You're going to try to get them to say something different?" Tom was still uncomfortable with Hingles answers.

"I can't do that, but I can try to put a different spin on it. I'm going to tie all the testimony together to form a consensus of what actually happened; and then offer an explanation why the quarrel does not constitute motive. With no motive, there's no intent and that's what the jury will remember?" He took another taste of wine. "Let me give you an example. John says he was pushed on top of Karen Burns. Its critical that we establish that he was, so he doesn't come off as some kind of playboy."

"Mr. Hingle," Katherine put down her fork and looked into his eyes. "How do you really feel about this? Are you going to be able to save my son?"

"I think we're going to be alright." Hingle hated the question. "A lot will depend on John. His testimony will sway the jury one way or the other." The three continued their conversation through coffee and Hingle's Crème Brule. As they left the restaurant Tom and Katherine understood better what Hingle was trying to do, but neither could deny the uneasy feeling in the pit of their stomachs. It was a feeling not caused by Emeril's skimpy meal. It was eight o' clock. Tom did not look forward to the trip back to Bay St. Louis.

CHAPTER 28

"Mr. Roberts, this is Detective Don Crawford with the Mississippi State Police." Fred Roberts was not expecting the call, and had to think for a moment. He had forgotten the name of the police detective who met with him after his daughter's accident. He had been out of the country when she and a friend were tragically killed in a hit and run on their way home from school. When he arrived home from a Germany business trip two days after the accident, it was this Detective Crawford who broke the news to him. That was almost six months ago and he still could not get over her death. All of her personal effects recovered from the scene were still neatly piled on her bed undisturbed since the day Fred placed them there. He could not bring himself to go through them.

"Oh Yes, Detective, I remember you. How are you doing?"

"I'm just fine Mr. Roberts. Listen, the last time we talked, I told you I would try to keep you informed on the disposition of your daughter's case." He paused.

"Yes, I remember. Thank you for calling."

"Well I apologize for not getting back sooner but I'm afraid this has been a real strange one. This guy who killed your daughter and Allison McKay turns out to be an illegal alien. We had a God-awful time trying to figure out who he was. He wouldn't give us any information. Anyway, he came into the country under some false pretense from Iran and tried to get asylum to stay. But that didn't work, and he was in the process of being deported when he disappeared. Apparently he was on the run and hiding out in our area when the accident happened."

"So what's going to happen to him?" Fred didn't care if it was an accident. He wanted this son of a bitch to know that in this country you pay when you take the lives of two young girls, and run away.

"Well, that's why I'm calling. He's been tried and convicted of vehicular manslaughter, and because he gave us such a hard time the judge threw the book at him. He's been sentenced to ten years, and when he gets out he will be sent back to where he came from."

"Ten years for two lives?"

"Yeah, but wait a minute." Crawford interrupted. "It may not be over yet. He's still being investigated. Seems this guy has some connections with some known Islamic terrorist groups in the country. He may have been part of a much bigger network that legally establishes operatives in the country. Then they participate in all kinds of subversive activity against the government. I understand these guys are fanatical in carrying out their objectives. Anyway, the Feds have taken over the case, and if they tie him into that, he'll never see old Saddam Hussein again."

"Well I hope they do." Fred was angry. "Who is the son of a bitch anyway? What's his name?"

"Oh Christ," Crawford hesitated. "I got his name here, but I'll be damned if I can say it. Looks like Abdul Rab-bin-ni, Rabbinni. That's the name he is using. Who knows what his real name is? Anyway, just following up. I knew you'd want to know."

"Thank you Detective. I appreciate your making the effort. I feel a little better knowing this guy's in prison, even though it's a small price to pay. Thanks again."

"No problem. You need anything else, be sure and call me."

"I will, thanks again."

CHAPTER 29

Hingle was not an early riser, if he could help it, but he was up at five-thirty on this the first day of his defense argument. He had not slept well; partly because of his concerns about the trial, but mostly because of the greasy gumbo that he tasted all night long. As he arrived at the office, he wished he were as confident about the outcome of the trial as he portrayed to the Stevens'.

He took about an hour to review his notes and set out for the court-house, where he had scheduled an early meeting with his client. John would want to know about the meeting he had with his parents. Hingle also wanted to prepare him for the days events.

Court reconvened at nine o'clock, and Hingle began immediately trying to undue the damage that had been done in the days before. He called Martin Feeny.

"Good morning, Mr. Feeny." Hingle assumed a friendly, laid back, good old, southern country boy attitude that had become his trade-mark in the courtroom. "I wanted to ask you a few more questions about the incident in John Stevens's apartment, if you don't mind."

"Sure, I don't mind."

"You and John were good friends weren't you?"

"Oh, yeah. All through school we were drinking buddies."

"He was your drinking buddy on graduation night wasn't he?"

"Yeah, we did some drinking that night."

"Can you recall for us how much you had to drink that night?"

Stern objected. "Irrelevant, Your Honor. How much Mr. Feeny had to drink has no bearing on the case." The Judge addressed Hingle. "Where are you going with this?"

"Your Honor, It goes to establishing the condition of the defendant on the evening in question. Mr. Feeny and Mr. Stevens were drinking together all night."

"The condition of this witness has nothing to do with the condition of the defendant. The objection is sustained." Hingle returned to his notes, trying not to show his disappointment.

"You testified that when you returned to Mr. Stevens apartment, you and he started fooling around with the girls. This was unusual behavior for the two of you wasn't it?"

"No, not really, I mean we were just fooling around. We were all feeling good, and having a little fun. The girls got a little upset and we stopped it. Actually, Mary stopped it, when she threw the water."

"Now, you testified that Miss Simmons threw water at you and Mr. Stevens and Miss Burns when she saw Mr. Stevens on top of Miss Burns on the couch. Can you tell us how Mr. Stevens came to be on top of Miss Burns?"

"Excuse me?"

"How did he get there? What happened just before he was on top of her?" Hingle had to establish that John was pushed.

"Hell, I don't know. I was coming out of the bathroom and there they were."

"You were in the bathroom?"

"That's right."

"But, you didn't say anything about being in the bathroom. You testified that when you saw John on the couch with Karen, you approached Mary." Hingle was beginning to sweat.

"That's right, but that was after I came out of the bathroom."

"And, you didn't see anybody push John?"

"No, I didn't see that." Feeny shook his head. "It could have happened though. All I saw was John and Karen kissing on the couch when I came out."

"Did you see Miss Courtney Roberts when you came out of the bathroom?" Hingle pursued.

"Yes, Courtney was standing in the kitchen when I came out."

"Is it possible that she could have pushed John?"

"Your Honor," Stern did not even bother to stand. "the witness has already testified that he did not see anyone push the defendant. I object to this continued line of questioning."

"Sustained." Judge Quinton was growing impatient. "Mr. Hingle I assume that you intend to recall these witnesses because you think they have something to add to these proceedings. I am allowing it at the discretion of the court for the time being, but I urge you to get on with it so as not to waste the courts time."

"Yes, Your Honor. All right, Mr. Feeny," Hingle again shifted his approach trying desperately not to show his frustration. "isn't it true that John Stevens was carrying on that evening with the girls in the apartment and especially with Karen Burns because he had had too much to drink, and that's what upset Mary Simmons so much?"

"Certainly, Mary got upset when he was on the couch with Karen, but I don't know if it was because he had too much to drink. Like I said before, I had as much as he did." Hingle had nowhere else to go with Feeny. He then made a final attempt to solicit some positive testimony.

"Do you think that John Stevens was capable of murdering Mary Simmons?"

"Objection, calls for speculation." This time Stern was more forceful.

"Sustained. Mr. Hingle, you are pushing my limits"

"Yes, Your Honor, I have no further questions of this witness." Stern remained in his seat trying to give the impression that Hingle's recall was obviously non-productive, and a waste of time.

"No questions."

"In that case," The judge said, picking up his files. "we'll break for lunch."

CHAPTER 30

Hingle had lunch by himself. He needed to think. Feeny was his best shot to establish the extent of John's drunkenness and to minimize the importance of the argument. He had accomplished neither, and managed to upset the judge while trying. He knew that he needed to get some points on the board quickly; and when he returned from lunch he refocused on those two objectives.

"Defense calls Karen Burns." By now Karen Burns was not a happy witness. She testified initially, thinking that she could help John; but she had no idea that her own reputation would get dragged through the mud while doing it. Stern made her sound like a cheap hooker, and she was not going to let that happen again. The judge reminded her that she was still under oath as Hingle approached her.

"Good morning Miss Burns, you testified that you thought John Stevens and Mary Simmons were in love. Isn't that true?" Hingle crossed his fingers.

"Yes, I believe they were."

"Well, wouldn't it be inconsistent and unusual behavior for someone who was in love to be romantically carrying on with someone else in front of the one he was supposed to be in love with?"

"Yes, I suppose so, but we were not exactly carrying on. It just happened, and Mary got upset."

"Well, that's what I'm trying to understand here. Can you tell us how it just happened? I mean, how did you and John come to be on that couch?"

"John was in the kitchen with Mary and Courtney Roberts." Karen welcomed the opportunity to clear up this point. "I was on the couch with Feeny, when Feeny got up to go to the bathroom. The next thing I know, John comes over the back of the couch and pulls me down onto the cushions. Obviously, I was surprised and we started laughing. We were all acting pretty silly by then. Then he kissed me; and that was pretty nice. So, I kissed him back."

"Just a minute, Miss Burns." Hingle interrupted. "Didn't you see Courtney Roberts push John, which caused him to fall over the couch onto you?"

"Is that what happened?"

"I'm asking you, Miss Burns. Didn't you see that?" Hingle was trying not to badger the witness, but his patience was wearing thin.

"Well I don't know if that happened, but I wouldn't have seen it anyway."

"Why is that?" Hingle hated to ask.

"Because the couch is between the kitchen and the living room, facing the living room, so my back was toward the kitchen." Karen was making little gestures with her hands trying to illustrate the position of the couch. Hingle pretended to be interested in the gestures; but his mind was working frantically.

"Let's go back a little bit. You said a few minutes ago that when John landed on the couch, you were all acting pretty silly. What did you mean by that. Why were you all acting silly?"

"Because we had been drinking since about eight o' clock, wine, beer, shots. That's why everything got blown out of proportion."

"And Mr. Stevens was drinking also?"

"Sure, that's what started it all. When he starts drinking, he gets all lovey and huggy. When we were dating he used to get like that a lot."

"So would you say that when he's drinking, his behavior is not normal?" Hingle thought he might be gaining a little ground.

"Well, of course he's not normal, when he's drinking; but who is. We all act like assholes when we drink, especially in this city. Whoops, I'm sorry, Judge. I didn't mean to say that in court." Judge Quinton accepted the apology, and tried to refrain from smiling at her astute observation.

"That may be true Miss Burns," Hingle did not appreciate the muted laughter in the courtroom. "but, isn't it also true that John Stevens drank more that night than he usually does?"

"Yes, I think he may have, but he had just gotten out of law school. There was certainly cause for celebration. Don't you think?"

"I certainly could not disagree with that, but, isn't that why he started kissing you and why he called the girl he loved a bitch" Hingle needed this one badly.

"Yes, I suppose so. I don't think he would have acted like that if he wasn't drinking."

"No More question, Your Honor." Hingle quickly sat down like a little boy who had stolen a cookie. But, his elation was short lived.

Stern approached the witness. "Miss Burns had you ever been with Mr. Stevens when he drank as much as he did on the night in question."

"Yes several times—after exams—on the weekends—during Mardi Gras."

"And during those times did you ever see him get violent?"

"No, never."

"Did he ever threaten you or hurt you in any way while you were dating him."

"No."

"No more questions?" As Stern sat down, Hingle was scratching feverishly on his note pad, but he was writing nothing. The nervous habit had been with him since law school and usually was a good indication that he was in trouble. With no new brainstorms, he decided to stay with his plan and recalled Patrick Healy. He spent some time reacquainting the jury with Healy's relationship with Stevens, and then focused on his objectives.

"Mr. Healy, you had been out with all of the people who attended the party at John Stevens's apartment on numerous occasions isn't that true?"

"Yes. We used to get together quite a bit."

"You were all good friends weren't you?"

"Yes"

"You had fun together; respected each other?"

"Yes, I would say so. We all got along very well."

"Now, on the night in question, you testified that a fight broke out in John Steven's apartment. You also said that when you and Mr. Churchill saw what was going on, you decided to leave. Is that right?"

"Yes, that's right."

"I was wondering Mr. Healy, if these were your good friend's, why you didn't stay to break up the fight. Weren't you concerned?" Hingle turned and faced the jury.

"I guess maybe we should have, but, hell, Church and I had been drinking too. We didn't want to get involved. Besides, we didn't really think it would amount to much. Everybody was just acting stupid. We thought they'd all forget about the whole thing by morning."

"So would you say that John Stevens was acting the way he did that night basically because he had too much to drink?"

"Yes I guess you could say that. I don't think the whole thing would have happened if we hadn't been drinking."

"And in your opinion, the quarrel was nothing. You thought it would blow over by morning. Didn't you say that?"

"Yes."

Hingle was satisfied. He turned the witness over to Stern. Stern approached the witness.

"Mr. Healy did John Stevens have any more to drink that night than you?"

"No, I don't think so. Not really."

"And did you kill anybody that night?" Stern knew now where Hingle was going and he wasn't going to give an inch.

"That's irrelevant, Your Honor." Hingle objected.

"Mr. Healy is not on trial here, Mr. Stern". The Judge was not amused. "Objection sustained."

"I withdrawn the question, and have no more for the witness." Stern smiled at Hingle as he sat down.

CHAPTER 31

Hingle decided it was time for a change of pace. He called Doctor Roland Caldwell, and took his time establishing the doctor as an expert in the study and treatment of alcoholism. The doctor had written several respected articles on the subject and ran a clinic that was recognized for is outstanding work in the field. He also made an excellent expert witness. He was tall with just enough gray hair at the temples to accent his well-trimmed mustache. Stern did not challenge the doctor's credentials.

"Doctor Caldwell," Hingle asked, satisfied that the jury was impressed with his witness's expertise. "can you tell us in layman's terms what happens to us when we drink to much?"

"No, I don't think I can." Hingle's jaw dropped. "What I mean is alcohol effects different people in different ways. Some people get happy when they drink, others get angry, and there's a whole range of emotions in between. Now, if you are asking about the physical changes to the body brought on by alcohol, I can be more specific."

"Alright, let's talk about those physical changes." Hingle relaxed a little bit.

"Well, alcohol dulls the senses. It retards motor skills and interferes with the ability to hear, think and speak clearly. It slows the brains capacity to understand and process information. This leads to confusion and disorientation. The confusion and disorientation is what causes different people to act differently while intoxicated. Some get happy; some get angry. Others may get depressed. Prolonged abuse of alcohol will begin to break down the body's organs such as the liver and pancreas and that can lead to chronic illness and death."

"So too much alcohol can make us act abnormally, make us do things we would not do while sober. Is that correct?"

"Not exactly, too much alcohol does not really make us do anything." Hingle nodded nervously. "More accurately, it removes the inhibitions and self-discipline that prevents us from speaking or acting in certain inappropriate ways under normal circumstances. In a sense, it allows us to behave in ways that are alien to our normal conduct. This is the result of the confusion and disorientation that I spoke about. For example, when people are sober, they know they should not drive a car while intoxicated, but when they get drunk, they lose that good judgment and drive anyway." Doctor Caldwell turned toward the jury. "You have heard people referred to as **happy drunks**, or **mean drunks**. Ironically these people exhibit behavior when intoxicated that is quite opposite to their normal personalities. In other words behavior that is suppressed under normal circumstances often emerges when the person is intoxicated."

"What do you mean by suppressed behavior?" This troubled Hingle.

"Let me give you another example. I have a friend who loves to sing. In fact, he is quite good at it. But, he is too embarrassed to sing in public under normal circumstances. So, he goes to the local Karaoke Bar, has a few drinks, and then you can't get him off the stage. Some people harbor hated that they keep suppressed until they drink, and then it erupts. That is a common occurrence that often results in violence."

"So is it possible," Hingle wanted to reinforce this point. "for some-one actually to kill a person while in this state of confusion and disori-entation that you talked about?"

"Sure it happens ever day on our highways. Whenever people inter-act with others while not in full control of their faculties, there is a potential to create a dangerous and sometimes deadly situations for themselves or others." That was not exactly the answer Hingle wanted, but he let it stand for the moment. He wanted to move on to the ques-tion of John's condition.

"Doctor can you tell us how much alcohol one needs to consume before reaching this state of confusion and disorientation that you speak of?"

"Well, there again alcohol can effect different people in different ways. Most states consider someone to be legally drunk if his blood alcohol level is, at or above point one- five. In an average size person this normally occurs if he has consumed three ounces of alcohol or three drinks within an hour. I would point out, however, that being 'legally drunk' and 'falling down drunk' can be miles apart. Many people can appear to be perfectly normal while legally drunk."

"So if a person is legally drunk after three drinks, how many drinks would it take for him to become confused and disoriented?"

"Well, that occurs gradually as more alcohol is consumed, but gener-ally speaking, if the average size person continues to consume alcohol at the rate of three ounces and hour, he is going to be very drunk or unconscious within three hours."

"And by very drunk you mean unable to think or speak clearly; dis-oriented and confused; and subject to emotional highs and lows."

"Yes that's correct."

"And in this condition, a person would be inclined to say and do things that he would not do if he were sober or normal?"

"Yes, that's true."

"Your Honor," Hingle was pleased with this testimony. "No more questions." Stern remained seated reviewing his notes with his co-council, a young wrinkled-suited assistant who had been feverishly plowing through reference material. After a few moments he stood and approached the witness.

"Good afternoon, Doctor." He was quick to offer the professional courtesy that he reserved for witnesses he respected or feared."

"Good afternoon, Mr. Stern." The doctor braced himself for the cross-examination.

"Doctor, I'm interested in exploring further something you said about how people react when under the influence of alcohol. Assuming that someone has consumed enough alcohol to be in a state of 'confusion and disorientation', as you say, how are they inclined to behave?"

"What I said was that alcohol impedes the brain's ability to function normally in receiving and processing information; and that, after substantial alcohol ingestion, an intoxicated person loses self control and begins to act out and say things that he would not allow himself to say or do while sober."

"So am I correct in understanding that this unusual behavior that emerges when we are drunk is behavior that we already have some predisposition toward? What I mean is; if your friend did not enjoy singing, would he be inclined to get up and sing whenever he got drunk."

"No, probably not. That's not to say that he absolutely would not under certain conditions; but if, normally, he had no interest in singing, there would be no suppressed desire that would emerge while intoxicated."

"And you talked about people, who suppress hatred in normal life and act out that hatred when intoxicated."

"That's correct. In incidences of hate crimes, by supremacist groups, for example, the studies reveal that almost all of those convicted drank heavily before carrying out their crime. But, it wasn't the alcohol that made them do it. It was the alcohol that allowed them to do something that they were already predisposed to do." Doctor Caldwell gave another example. "A husband does not get drunk and just decides to beat up his wife. Typically he is driven by some pent up emotion that has developed within him over a period of time."

"So, Doctor, let me ask you this? Is it possible for someone with no predisposition toward hatred or violence to get so drunk that he would murder the women he loves." Stern went right for the jugular.

"Theoretically it is possible, but it is very unlikely. Ruling out accidental death or homicides committed in the heat of passion, it would be very unusual for someone, just because he was intoxicated, to kill a person whom he had no malice toward while sober."

"Thank you, Doctor. No more questions." Hingle was on his feet and anxious to redirect.

"Doctor, didn't you say that a person could get so drunk that he could lose control of his actions."

"Yes. That's true."

"And, isn't it possible that someone, severely intoxicated, could imagine things, hallucinate; and while hallucinating, kill someone?"

"Yes that's possible, but not probable, you see, hallucinations are usually the manifestations of something already in the mind. A fear that can be controlled while a person is sober can take on many forms while he is intoxicated. I've treated many veterans who have survived severe combat situations only to relive horrible experiences through alcohol induced hallucinations. But, again those are manifestations of deep rooted fears."

"I see." Hingle had entangled himself in a mess, with nowhere to go. Any more questions of the good doctor and he might be personally responsible for John's conviction. Reluctantly he had to let him go. "No more questions."

For the rest of the afternoon, Hingle called two college professors who spoke highly of John as both a student and person. There was very little interest in these witnesses on the part of the prosecution. For that matter, the jury seemed totally unimpressed with anything they had to say; and by the end of the day when the judge called for adjournment, Hingle felt that he was being drawn and quartered by his own witnesses.

CHAPTER 32

That evening Hingle reviewed the status of the case with his associates. He knew it was not going well and he was openly soliciting some ideas. The original strategy was not working. He depended on John's friends to verify that John was so drunk that he did not know what he was doing. Their testimony failed to do that. In fact their testimony, if anything, established that his client wasn't much more intoxicated than they were; and none of them had a problem getting home; no one but Mary Simmons that is.

Even if the witnesses had testified that John was totally ossified, and acting irrationally as he had hoped, Doctor Caldwell just about destroyed his argument that if John killed her, he did not know what he was doing. The doctor was very clear in saying that other than deaths caused by accidental negligence, or in the heat of passion, diminished culpability due to intoxication, was improbable. This was certainly no accident, and if John acted out of passion, then he knew what he was doing. Hingle had been foolish not to better prepare for this witness.

Without some solid basis for arguing that John's condition prevented him from knowing what he was doing, Hingle only had one avenue left, motive. He would have to convince a jury that John had no reason to kill Mary Simmons. He did his best through witness testimony to diminish the importance of the rift that John and Mary had; but that had not gone well either. The fact remained that the couple had a disagreement, which essentially broke up the party; and none of the witnesses could absolutely say that the fight did not continue to escalate after they left.

The character witnesses did as well as could be expected; but Hingle knew that their testimony alone was not enough to overcome the evidence. And then, of course, there was that evidence, the murder weapon with his client's handprints all over it. Maybe he should have challenged the forensics, but what could he do? Those prints where not going to go away.

All he had left was John. When he decided earlier to have him speak for himself, he thought that he would have some favorable prior witness testimony on the record to support him. Unfortunately, all the testimony actually did was strengthen Stern's case.

"Okay, He addressed the six associates who he had assembled in his conference room. They had listened intently as he summarized the case. "Anybody got any ideas?"

"Yeah, I got one." A pimply-faced junior associate seemed to find some humor in the situation. "Why don't we ask Quinton to release us from the case?" The more experienced lawyers, understanding the seriousness of the situation, did not appreciate his comment.

"I am serious, gentlemen, we are in trouble on this one." Hingle had no time for levity.

"Dan", Bill Barrone spoke up. "I know why you let the forensic testimony go, but in light of where this thing is now, should we take another look at that evidence. What about that knife? Can we cast some doubt on its being the actual murder weapon?"

"Or, can we establish that Stevens may have handled the weapon after the murder?" Another attorney suggested. "After all, if he was as drunk as he says, he could have done anything."

For what it was worth, Hingle now had the collective creative juices of his staff flowing. They brainstormed for more than an hour, dismissing one idea after another. In the end, an ominous silence came over the group, and Hingle realized that nothing helpful had come from the discussion. He was left with what he started with, John Steven's own testimony.

On Thursday morning he avoided contact with Tom Stevens, sending him a message that he would be tied up preparing John for his testimony. The fact was, he knew well that Tom was not happy with the previous days proceedings and wanted desperately to question him. Hingle had no plausible or slick answers this time. At five minutes to ten he entered the courtroom through the restricted backdoor, and after an obligatory nod at the Stevens', he busied himself with file folders.

"All Rise." Promptly at ten o' clock the bailiff called the courtroom to order and Judge Quinton took the bench.

"Good morning ladies and gentlemen. Mr. Hingle are you ready to proceed?"

"We are, Your Honor, thank you."

"Defense calls the defendant Mr. John Stevens." As he had appeared throughout the trial, John was well dressed in a dark blue suit and tie. He cleaned and shaved himself that morning as though his life depended on it. As he sat on the witness stand he looked every bit the bright, considerate young man that he folks knew him to be. "Mr. Stevens, do you mind if I call you John?" Hingle wanted to bring the jury as close to his client as possible.

"No, sir, that's fine."

"John, there's been some confusion as to what actually happened on the evening of May 7, 1998. Would you tell the jury in your own words everything you recall about that evening." Hingle took his seat as John began a painstaking narrative of every detail just as he had relived it a hundred times in his mind. He held the jury spellbound as he told them how he and Mary met, how they fell in love. He talked about the ring he had purchased for her. He took them through the dinner at Café Giovanni; the walk through the Quarter; the streetcar ride, and then the details of the gathering at his apartment. He was very clear about how Courtney Roberts pushed him away when he was kissing her, and how he fell over the couch on to Karen Burns. He seemed to be apologizing to the court for his behavior and for being so drunk.

"The last thing I remember, I was on the floor looking up at Karen Burns and Martin Feeny. Karen was yelling at Marty, as they were leaving. I must have fallen asleep or passed out on the floor at that point. After that, I woke up in the bathroom. I was in the tub. I guess I fell into the tub somehow. I don't remember doing that. My head was bleeding. I got out of the tub and I got sick. Then I went into the kitchen and that's when I found Mary." John bowed his head. "And, that's all I remember." Hingle was now approaching his witness.

"John, do you recall what you had to drink at dinner?"

"Yes, we all decided to drink wine, Merlot. There were eight of us and we ordered four bottles during dinner. I remember having three glasses."

"Did you drink anything before dinner?"

"No"

"Now, when you left the restaurant and walked through the French Quarter what did you drink?"

"Well, we bought some beer. Large beers in twenty-four once cups. I drank one of those on the way to the street car, and Mary couldn't finish half of hers so she gave it to me and I drank that too."

"And, you mentioned that you and Mr. Feeny had some Jack Daniels. Is that correct?"

"Yes, Feeny had a pint of Jack Daniels. He had been taking shots, and he offered me some on the streetcar. I believe I took three drinks."

"How were you feeling at that time?"

"I guess I was feeling pretty good. I mean we were having a good time and I wasn't thinking too much about what I was drinking. I was pretty happy about graduating."

"So, when you arrived at the apartment you were all still in a good mood, weren't you?"

"Yes, Feeny and I finished the Jack Daniels while we were drinking beer."

"How many beers did you have before you passed out?" Hingle looked at John, in a way that reassured him that his testimony was going well.

"I really can't say for sure, but I think I had at least four more in the apartment."

"Now, John let me ask you this. Do you recall ever being as intoxicated as you were on the night of your graduation?"

"No, sir. I never passed out before, and I was never as sick as I was the day after." Hingle was satisfied that he had gone as far as he could with the drinking, and changed direction.

"John, you loved Mary Simmons didn't you?"

"Yes, I did, very much. I was going to ask her to marry me. I was going to give her a ring."

"But you had a fight with her on that evening didn't you?" Hingle wanted to get past this question on his terms.

"It wasn't really a fight." John was pleading for understanding. "Mary and I never had a fight. I was just acting stupid and she got mad at me. I was wrong. I got her upset by fooling with the other girls. And, then when she threw the water, she surprised me and I said something stupid. I know I called her a bitch, and I was very sorry I did. I know I hurt her when I said that. I never talked to her like that before. I was drunk. That's all. I can't explain it any other way. I was drunk and I am so sorry, but I would never hurt her." Hingle believed him and he knew the jury was impressed with his sincerity. He took a position directly in front of the witness, and asked the inevitable question.

"John, did you kill Mary Simmons?"

"Oh God, I couldn't have killed her. How could I? I loved her."

"No more questions." It was close to twelve o'clock. John had been testifying for almost three hours. Judge Quinton looked around his courtroom and realized that John's testimony had deeply moved most in attendance. He himself needed a break before proceeding.

"Ladies and Gentlemen, it has been a long morning. I am going to adjourn at this time. Please be prepared to reconvene at two o'clock."

CHAPTER 33

Fred Roberts had been thinking about his daughter since the phone call from Detective Crawford. Even though their lives had taken them in different directions most of the time, he and Courtney always enjoyed the time they spent together. Fred looked forward to her vacations and home visits. He always tried to arrange his schedule so that he could spend some quality time with his daughter. His trip to Germany had been unavoidable, and he still deeply regretted having missed her graduation. And now, he missed her young spirit and her refreshing frankness whenever they talked. As the time continued to pass, he realized even more how much he had lost, and how empty his life had become.

It was time now for him to face the fact that Courtney was not coming home again. He stood in her bedroom looking at the pile of boxes, suitcases, and clothing that remained as he had placed it six months earlier. He separated most of the clothing and hung it in her closet, to deal with another day. He then emptied the suitcases, and folded the rest of her garments into neat piles. The boxes contained an assortment of books and notebooks that Courtney apparently had reason to keep. He flipped through the law books and thought what a tragedy his daughter's death really was. She was so bright, with such great potential.

He stacked the books in the bookcase he'd built to hold the law library that Courtney began accumulating in her first year. Her notebooks were neatly kept. He decided to hold on to those also. In the corner of one carton was a leather secretary. He opened it and began to read some entries from the chronicle of his daughter's life, as she kept it, from day to day, throughout her senior year. As he read her small neatly handwritten entries, he imagined her keeping the appointments with friends, professors, her dentist, and others who were part of her life. It made him feel nearer to her. He touched the soft leather to his face and then set the secretary aside to be read later, at times, when he missed her most.

As he unpacked the miscellaneous junk that Courtney had collected for reasons known only to her, he came across a small box wrapped in brown paper. It was addressed to Mr. John Stevens in Bay St. Louis, Mississippi. She had hand written *personal* on the package. He bounced the small box from hand to hand wondering what importance it may have had in his daughter's life. Finally, overcoming the urge to open it, he put it with the leather secretary. He would forward it to Mr. Stevens in the morning.

Fred continued to sort out those things that he would donate to St. Vincent De Paul. He would of course call Courtney's mother before disposing of anything. Although he had not seen her since the funeral, there was no hostility between them and they did whatever they could to help each other deal with their terrible mutual loss. With everything accounted for, he picked up the secretary and the little box, and taking a final look around the room, he turned out the light and closed the door.

Later that evening Fred warmed up some spaghetti and had dinner by himself. As he ate he thought again about his daughter's secretary, and when he finished cleaning up the few dirty dishes, he retired to the den to read through some of her entries. The little notes that Courtney wrote to herself in the margins amused him; and he was impressed with the busy life she lived while at school. There were school classes; there were lecture dates; there were dates with friends; and there were meetings with clients whom she represented through the Tulane Law Clinic. One of these entries caught his attention.

March 20, 1998, 10:00 AM

Law Clinic

Meet with Mary regarding Rabbinni

There was something about Rabbinni that sounded familiar to him, but he could not recall why. Had Courtney introduced him to a professor with that name? Who was Mary? It was getting late and Fred decided it was time to turn in, but like a melody that sticks in the brain the name Rabbinni echoed in his mind until he finally fell asleep.

CHAPTER 34

The two-hour lunch break only served to heighten the anxiety in the courtroom. John and Hingle spent the time anticipating Stern's cross-examination. Tom and Katherine went to the cafeteria and tried to eat a vending machine sandwich. They could not. They both felt John had handled himself well on the stand. The parents could not believe that anyone would think their son was guilty, but they realized that their opinion didn't count. The two hours seemed like an eternity, and while they did not look forward to the afternoon session they were anxious to get on with it. Prosecutor Stern had, of course, used the lunch break well, and he wasted no time going after his witness, when court resumed at two.

"Mr. Stevens, do you recognize this knife?" He handed him the exhibit. John was startled by the knife and the question.

"Yes, its part of a set that I have in my kitchen."

"It's your knife isn't it?"

"Yes, I said that."

"And we've already established that those are your finger prints, haven't we?"

"Yes, but I don't know how that happened?"

"You have no idea how your full hand print came to be on the blood stained handle of the knife that slaughtered Mary Simmons? Is that what you want this jury to believe?" Stern left the murder weapon with John as he turned to the jury for a reaction.

"Yes, Sir, I do not remember how that happened." John set the knife down in front of him on the witness stand.

"You and Ms. Simmons saw quite a bit of each other during you last year of law school, is that right?"

"Yes we did?" John went on nervously talking about his relationship with Mary until he had nothing else to say. Stern did not interrupt until he stopped.

"And, isn't it true that you used to fight all the time?"

"No, that's not true." John was upset by the allegation. "We never fought about anything. That night in my apartment was the only time we ever had any kind of a disagreement."

"You mean to tell this court that you didn't have a deep seeded contempt for Mary Simmons?"

"Contempt?" John responded, as Stern knew he would. "I loved Mary. Why would I have any contempt for her."

"Well, maybe contempt is the wrong word, but weren't there a lot of little things about her that you couldn't stand."

"No. There was nothing about her that I didn't love. I couldn't wait to see her. I couldn't wait to be with her whenever I could." John was looking at Mary's parents, seated in the fourth row.

"So, you don't believe that somewhere in your subconscious you were suppressing a desire to inflict bodily harm to Mary Simmons do you?"

"I object, Your Honor." Hingle finally saw what Stern was doing. "Your Honor, neither the prosecutor nor the witness is trained in matters of the mind, nor is either capable of making such observations."

"Your Honor," Stern interrupted. "This is a subject introduced by the defense's own expert. I am merely following up and asking the defendant if he harbored any bad feelings toward the victim. He doesn't have to be a psychiatrist to answer that."

"I'll allow it." Quinton ruled. "You may answer the question."

John didn't seem to understand what the prosecutor was trying to do, but he did know the answer to the question and he wasted no words delivering it. "No way, I had nothing but love and respect for Mary Simmons whether conscious or subconscious. I never thought about hurting her in any way."

"Well, then can you tell us why you got so angry with her that night, when you called her a bitch?" Stern turned again to watch the jury's reaction.

"I told you she surprised us when she threw the water. She got Karen and me all wet. We were embarrassed. I just reacted. I didn't really mean what I said."

"So she embarrassed you in front of your former girlfriend, and all of your buddies, is that what happened?"

"No". He was uncertain how to answer. "Well, yes I guess you can say that. But it was just a quick reaction. I didn't think about what I was saying."

"I understand Mr. Stevens, you acted impulsively didn't you?"

"Yes, I guess so."

"And after all your friends left and you and Mary Simmons were alone you got mad and acted impulsively again didn't you?"

"No, I don't remember that."

"You started thinking again about how she had embarrassed you; and you got angry again. You argued and you impulsively killed her with that knife, which is still covered with her blood and your finger-prints. Isn't that what really happened?"

"No. That's a lie. That could not have happened."

"You like to drink don't you Mr. Stevens?"

"What do you mean?"

"Well, I mean you were an all American college boy living in New Orleans. You've seen your share of Mardi Gras parties, and you drink. Wouldn't you say?"

"Yes, but not anymore than anyone else."

"I'm sorry. Stern approached John. "I didn't hear what you just said."

"I said yes. I partied and I drank, but not any more than anyone else. It was just a part of our social life."

"Oh, so you and your friends used to fall down drunk and pass out all over New Orleans as part of your social life, is that correct?" Stern baited him.

"No, that's not true." John looked at his parents. "I never drank like that. I was the one who made sure everyone else was okay. I made sure everyone got home all right. I drank, yes, but I'm no drunk. I can control myself." Hingle put his head in his hands as John's words echoed through the courtroom. Stern flipped through some papers on the prosecution table, and waited for the appropriate moment to begin again.

"Mr. Stevens, the coroner has fixed the time of Ms. Simmon's death at about 2:00 A.M. Monday morning May 8th. Can you tell us where you where at that time?"

"I'm not sure where I was exactly. After I passed out on the floor, I don't know how I got to the bathroom, where I woke up."

"So, is it safe to say that you were either laying on the kitchen floor, or you were in the bathroom just off the kitchen?"

"Yes, I guess so. I don't know where else I could have been." John shifted in his seat. Stern now approached the witness stand and took the knife that had been resting in front of the witness during his questioning.

"You were in the courtroom when the coroner described the brutal attack on Ms. Simmons, were you not?"

"Yes."

"And did you hear him say that she was stabbed eighteen times, as she struggled for her life, under a vicious attack?"

"Yes, I did."

"Mr. Stevens", Stern looked directly into John's eyes. "do you really expect this jury to believe that while Mary Simmons was fighting for her life, you slept through that slaughter less than fifteen feet away?"

"Yes. John tried to visualize that terrible scene. "I mean I don't know. I don't know where I was, or what I did. I didn't hear anything. I don't remember any of it." Stern turned quickly and raised his voice as he walked toward the jury.

"You didn't hear her struggling with an attacker, because there was no attacker." He turned again and pointed his finger at John. "You don't remember that struggle because it didn't happen. It didn't happen, because you killed Mary Simmons, with this knife." He raised the knife above his head in a threatening manner for the benefit of the jury. "That's what really happened, and that's what you do remember. Isn't it?"

"Objection."

"Overruled."

"No. No." John was confused. "I don't know what happened."

"No more questions." Anxious to bring an end to the agony, Hingle quickly stood up.

"The defense rests, your Honor." There was nothing left...nowhere else to go. He would have to try to reconstruct his defense during his closing statement.

"Okay, Ladies and Gentlemen," Judge Quinton addressed the jury. "the next stage of this trial will involve the closing statements from the prosecution and defense attorneys. I would expect that both attorneys will require some time to summarize their cases. Therefore, I am going to adjourn for today, so that you may hear both statements in the morning. I would also expect that the case will be given to you for deliberation tomorrow afternoon. I would remind you again that you are to discuss this case with no one. Thank you."

CHAPTER 35

The following morning, Matt Stevens waited anxiously for his parents outside the courtroom. They did not expect him, even though he said he would try to make the trial on Friday. The truth was he did not know, himself, whether he would attend until late last night, when he decided to catch an early flight.

As the second floor elevator doors opened, he saw his mother and dad step out. They looked tired. His mother especially seemed much older than when he'd last seen her. Her face brightened as she looked toward the courtroom and saw her oldest son.

"Look, Tom, Matt came." She quickened her steps over the marble floor to greet her son. They embraced, and she held on to him as though she feared someone would take him from her.

"Matt", Tom greeted him. "I am so glad you came. It will mean a lot to John."

"Yes, well I'm sorry I've not been more supportive, but it's been hard. Can we get a cup of coffee some where?"

They went to the cafeteria, where Tom and Katherine filled in Matt on the week's proceedings.

"So this is the big day." Katherine said nervously. "The lawyers are going to conclude and the jury will decide if John is innocent."

Matt looked at his mother and could feel her anxiety "It's going to be all right, Mom. I'm sure of it. John is innocent." Katherine nodded.

"We better take our seats." Tom glanced at the clock. "The courtroom fills up very fast."

He was right. Word must have gotten out that the jury would receive the case today. At eight o'clock Tom had trouble finding three seats together. By nine when the bailiff called for order in the courtroom, it was full.

"Mr. Hingle would you proceed with your summation, please." Judge Quinton anticipated a difficult day. Hingle approached the jury box.

"Good morning, Ladies and Gentlemen. There are a lot of things we don't understand in life, aren't there? But then, we are not expected to understand everything. That's why God, blessed each of us with common sense. Common sense to help us recognize when something just ain't right. Now, we may not know what happened on the morning of May 8, 1998; but our common sense tells us that there's something that just ain't right about this case against John Stevens. Let's examine some of the facts in this case. First and most importantly, contrary to what Mr. Stern may claim, Mr. Stevens has not confessed to killing anyone, and it would be wrong for you to proceed under that premise. He has quite honestly admitted that he does not know what happened to Ms. Simmons or himself on that evening and early morning. He has not denied committing this crime only because he cannot account for his actions at that time. Mr. Stevens has anguished over the death of Mary Simmons as much as anyone possibly could. But the simple fact is; he does not remember anything. And, the reason he does not remember is that this young man, who was not used to heavy drinking, seriously exceeded his limit on the evening of his graduation from law school, and got himself very, very drunk."

"Doctor Caldwell described how easy it is to lose control of our senses when under the influence of alcohol. Indeed the law says we are incapable of driving an automobile when we have imbibed only three ounces of alcohol. By the most conservative estimates, John Stevens drank at least three times that amount before he lost consciousness on Sunday night. To deny that he was not seriously under the influence of alcohol on that night is to turn our backs on the most critical evidence in this case."

"You all heard what his law professors had to say about the defendant, and you listened to John tell you in his own words what he remembered of that evening. Did that bright, young, God-fearing man sound like someone who would intentionally stab to death the women he loved? It just doesn't make sense, Ladies and Gentlemen. And if it doesn't make sense, it probably did not happen."

"Now, there are only two possible explanations of what happened to Mary Simmons. It is possible that, while in an alcohol-induced state of totally irrational behavior, John Stevens did something so terrible that it will haunt him for the rest of his life. If, God forbid, that happened, he is certainly responsible for her death, but he should not be convicted of committing a willful and intentional murder."

"But, what if it did not happen that way at all? There is another possibility. What if someone else is responsible for this crime?" Hingle walked slowly in front of the jury, making eye contact as he tried to plant a new idea in their minds. "I would ask you to consider this far more plausible scenario." He positioned himself before the jury.

"Early Monday morning while Mary Simmons is cleaning up and John lies passed out in the bedroom, an intruder enters the apartment.

He attacks and kills Ms. Simmons; but in doing so, he wakes John. A struggle follows. The bloody knife changes hands as John and the assailant fight their way into the bathroom, where John is pushed into the bathtub. He strikes his head on the soap dish and is knocked unconscious. The assailant seizes the opportunity to escape, and throws the knife into the tub as he flees."

"Now, Ladies and Gentlemen, I don't know if it happened that way, but it could have. None of us really knows. And, if he is guilty, John Stevens could have made up a story just like that to cover up his guilt. But he did not. All he says is he does not know what happened, and that's the truth. The law says that before you can find John Stevens guilty of second degree murder, you must know beyond a reasonable doubt that he killed Mary Simmons, and, more importantly, that he did it with willful intent. Ladies, and Gentlemen, any reasonable person knows that just does not make sense. And, if doesn't make sense, then it probably isn't true. Certainly there must be enough reasonable doubt in your minds that will allow you find this young man not guilty of willful and intentional murder, and to save him from spending the rest of his life in prison. Thank you." Before Hingle could return to the defense table, Stern was already on his feet anticipating Judge Quinton's directive.

"Mr. Stern."

"Thank you, Your Honor. Good morning, Ladies and Gentlemen." He was characteristically focused and intense. "There are indeed some confusing elements about this case. Aren't there? A lot of unanswered questions. We look at a young man like John Stevens and we wonder how he could have committed such a horrendous murder. Mr. Hingle wants you to believe that such a crime just couldn't happen. Well, my job, as prosecuting attorney, is not to speculate, but to present the evidence, so that you, the jury, can conclude for yourself what the facts are. The evidence in this case is crystal clear; and that irrefutable evidence leads us to two inescapable conclusions. One - Mary Simmons was brutally attacked and murdered in the early morning hours of May 8, 1998, in the apartment of John Stevens; and two - John Stevens committed that murder. Make no mistake about that. Mr. Hingle rightfully points out that at no time during the course of this trial did you hear John Stevens say he did not kill that girl. He said he couldn't have done it. He said he wouldn't have done it. He said he doesn't remember doing it. And, finally, he said he doesn't know what happened. Well, Ladies and Gentlemen, **he did it**. The fact that he and the victim fought prior to the murder, in the presence of witnesses, tells you **he did it**. His being in the apartment at the time of the crime tells you **he did it**. And his prints on the murder weapon emphatically tell you **he did it**."

"Now, Mr. Hingle over there, throughout this trial, has not been concerned whether or not his client killed Mary Simmons because he wants you to believe that Stevens was too drunk to know what he was doing, and therefore there was no intent. And consequently, he thinks you need to let him go free. His last minute attempt to introduce a mysterious intruder is ridiculous, and not supported by any evidence introduced in this trial. Such a scenario should be rejected outright, as a desperate attempt to bolster a flawed defense. You don't need to decide if John Stevens viciously killed Mary Stevens, ladies and gentlemen. We all know he did. The evidence confirms that. What you do need to decide, however, - and this is extremely important- is whether he did it willfully. In order to convict him of this crime you need to be convinced that, at the time he was plunging that knife into her body eighteen times, John Stevens intended to kill Mary Simmons. That's what we really need to talk about this morning. We need to closely examine that question of intent."

"Now, you all heard the esteemed Doctor Caldwell, a defense witness by the way, tell you about the effects of alcohol and why an intoxicated person might take the life of another. He said such an act might be an accident. Well, with eighteen stab wounds, we know that this brutal attack was no accident. He said an intoxicated person might kill while hallucinating, but he was quick to add that any such hallucinations would have to be the result of some deep-rooted fear or physiological disorder. There is no evidence that the defendant suffers from any such fear or disorder. The doctor also said that under the influence of alcohol, someone could kill out of suppressed anger, anger that comes to the surface when the alcohol provides the courage to act out the suppressed aggression. But Stevens, himself, told us that he harbored no such suppressed anger toward Mary Simmons. He loved everything about her, according to him. Remember what the doctor said, unless there was some predisposition to commit a violent act when sober, alcohol alone would not cause someone to do so. So, it would appear, by testimony of his own witness, that John Stevens had none of these preconditions that would result in a diminished capacity to understand what he was doing while attacking Mary Simmons." Stern stopped to let the jury absorb his conclusions.

"But, not withstanding the Doctors testimony, He continued. "we also have to ask ourselves, just how drunk was the defendant? I ask you to recall the testimony of the four witnesses who drank with John Stevens that night. None of them told you that Stevens was so drunk that he did not know what he was doing. In fact, they said he was not noticeably drunker than any of the others including his best drinking buddy Martin Feeny, who drank Jack Daniels with him. Isn't it interesting that none of those friends got so drunk that they passed out? On the contrary, they all left the party, and went home with no problem. In fact, Feeny and Karen Burns went to the neighborhood bar where they met David Churchill and Patrick Healy, and continued to drink before going home. John Stevens himself told you that he is not a drunk. He says he is a responsible drinker. He is the one, he said, who looks out for his friends when they are drinking. But, on this one specific night, he wants you to believe that he abandoned that customary responsible behavior, and drank himself into unconsciousness, and while in that state he unknowingly may have stabbed the victim eighteen times, until she was dead. Such a hypothesis insults the intelligence of every reasonable person." Stern paused again long enough for the jury to consider the validity of his logic.

"So why then, you have to ask, did John Stevens kill Mary Simmons? The answer may be hard to understand, but it's really quite simple. She pissed him off." His choice of words was intentional. "It started when she threw the water and embarrassed him in front of friends, but it didn't stop there. It escalated as the night went on. Karen Burns, the former girlfriend, no doubt was brought up again, and he got more upset. Mr. Feeny told you he had a temper. By two in the morning, it developed into a terrible fight, and Stevens finally ended it by stabbing Mary Stevens to death. He then went to the bathroom with the knife to clean himself up. That's when he fell into the tub and knocked himself out. And that's when, he developed the convenient case of amnesia that he would have you believe afflicts him to this day. Yes, John Stevens knew well what he was doing. He stabbed that girl over and over again until she was dead. He fully intended to kill her, and it would be a travesty if he were not held responsible for it. Each of you have the responsibility to see that he pays for his crime by returning a verdict of guilty of second degree murder as charged."

As he returned to the table, tears were running down Katherine Stevens's face. Tom's attention was riveted on the jury, as he tried to read their expressionless faces. Hingle sat in his chair, looking like someone had kicked him in the groin.

CHAPTER 36

By noontime, the judge had finished instructing the jury and retired them to deliberate the fate of John Stevens. Katherine was not feeling well and John decided to take a room at the Hampton Inn until the jury returned with a verdict. He had no idea how long that would be, but he convinced her to let him take her to the hotel to rest for an hour. Matt would stay at the courthouse to monitor the jury's progress, as best he could.

Hingle accompanied his client back to the holding room to await the verdict. He did what he could to comfort John, but he was visibly concerned that he had not successfully rebutted Stern's convincing argument. He paced nervously around the room.

"We are not going to win this, are we?" John sensed his concern.

"You never know what a jury will do." What else could Hingle say? "I think we made a strong presentation. Your testimony was very good. The witnesses did not help as much as I'd hoped, but I don't think they hurt us too much. It's that damn knife, John." Hingle was rehashing the entire trial in his mind.

John knew it looked bad, but he was preoccupied with Stern's closing statement. "Do you think it could have happened that way; the way he said? Do you think I might have killed her and developed amnesia when I hit my head?"

"You may have, but it makes little difference now."

"It makes a big difference to me. I still need to know what happened to her. If I killed her, I need to know that." John was exhausted from sleepless nights, and he could not fight the tears leaking down his face.

"John let's take this one step at a time. You need to stay strong. If things do not go well, we will appeal." John didn't seem to hear him.

Katherine woke after a much-needed nap, anxious to know if anything had happened while she slept. Nothing had. Tom sat nervously by the phone still waiting for Matt's call. Three hours had passed.

"I want to go back there, Tom. He's going to need us there."

"Okay." Tom didn't argue with her. He was torn between her needing more rest and wanting to be there when the jury returned. "Whenever you are ready."

Matt called his brother and sister from the courtroom. He knew they were both feeling very badly about their lack of support for the family. He understood their situations, and wanted them to know what was happening. He promised to call again after the verdict was returned.

At four-thirty the jury asked for a clarification of Doctor Caldwell's testimony. It seemed to them that both attorneys had used the same testimony to argue their cases, and the jury wanted to review what he actually said. They were also struggling with the possibility that Stevens may not have committed the crime despite the undeniable evidence to the contrary. To some of the members, Hingle's common sense argument hit home. It seemed so improbable that John could have killed the girl he obviously loved.

By six o'clock, Judge Quinton was beginning to wonder if a verdict might be forthcoming, and he inquired as to the jury's progress. In a note back to him, the foreman advised that he thought they were close. At seven they had indeed reached a verdict.

In spite of the late hour, the courtroom filled up rapidly when word of the pending verdict flooded the courthouse. Tom, Katherine and Matt, who all sat alone for most of the afternoon, were now suddenly surrounded by strangers, as a carnival like excitement overtook the courtroom.

Noticeably absent were Mr. and Mrs. Simmons. They had faithfully attended every session, but now neither felt a compulsion to be present for the verdict. Whatever it might be, they realized, it would not bring Mary back, and by now they had overcome any ill feelings that they may have had toward John Stevens. It was clear to them that if he killed their daughter, he had to have been acting under some uncontrollable influence, and they at least had concluded that their daughter's death was not the result of his willful intent to kill her. They had decided to let the jury make the legal decision, but as for them, they had had enough and wanted only to return home to try to remember the good things about a daughter who, for reasons known only to God, had been taken away from them.

Hingle and John entered from the rear of the courtroom, followed shortly after by Judge Quinton. When the courtroom was silenced, the jury was brought in. Courtroom artists scratched feverishly at their sketchpads trying to capture the tension in the air. Whispers began hissing through the spectators as they tried to read the verdict on the faces of the jurymen. Quinton waited for the silence that the moment demanded.

"Mr. Foreman, I understand that you have reached a verdict."

"We have, Your Honor." The bailiff relieved the foreman of the scrap of paper that weighed heavily in his hand, and passed it to the judge. Judge Quinton examined the paper with far more attention than he needed to understand its few written words. Passing it to the bailiff, he directed him to read the verdict out load.

"In the matter of the State of Louisiana versus John Andrew Stevens, we find the defendant guilty of murder in the second degree, as charged."

The courtroom erupted in a cacophony of confusion and chaos. The guards descended on John and quickly ushered him back through the rear door. Hingle remained in is seat, unable to move. Tom was angrily making his way to the front of the courtroom, while Matt pulled on his arm, trying to calm him down. Frenzied reporters rushed the lawyers, trying to overhear a few words that would embellish their headlines.

Through all the turmoil no one noticed that Katherine had not reacted to the news. She remained in her seat, seemingly unaffected by the excitement around her. No one could tell that she had sustained a massive coronary when the verdict was read. Tom and Matt had been so focused on the bailiff, they were not aware of Katherine's condition. As the crowd moved frantically throughout the courtroom, Katherine slumped forward. Her body slipped slowly under the bench. For her the ordeal was now over.

CHAPTER 37

It was a cool damp Saturday morning in the small historic Bay St. Louis cemetery. Tom stood looking down at the silver gray casket, as a light drizzle began to form shiny beads on its polished surface. He could not remember selecting it. Artificial grass covered the mounds of dirt; and flowers, rushed from the funeral home, were neatly arranged around the gravesite.

There had been a wake, and a Catholic Mass. An endless line of friends and family had filed passed the open casket, expressing their sympathies to Tom and the family. The family, except for John, now stood next to Tom, as the priest sprinkled holy water over the casket and recited prayers, intended to comfort the bereaved.

As he raised his head and looked out over the cemetery's stone markers, Tom began to doubt the reality of the moment. The mist in the air added to the surrealism. Was this real? Had he really lost both his son and his wife within the last few days? Katherine's death alone, after 36 years of marriage, would have been devastating to him; but with the events of the last six months and finally John's conviction, Tom was beginning to wonder if he were trapped in some terrible nightmare. Martha's sobbing made him realize that it was all very real. He put his arm around her.

Michael and Kimberly held each other, both overwhelmed by grief and guilt. Matt, with his wife at his side, stood by his father.

One by one, other relatives and friends placed flowers on the casket and quietly walked to their automobiles. There would be no customary reception after the funeral. Tom appreciated the support, but the thought of John sitting alone in a cell while his mother was lowered into her grave, made it impossible for him to entertain anyone. Matt took Martha to the car. Mike and Kimberly lingered, wishing there was some way they could tell Katherine how sorry they were for not being there when she needed them most. They finally returned to the car, leaving their father standing alone in the rain.

He stood, eyes fixed on the casket, for another twenty minutes remembering the women who had become such a part of him. Many years before their spirits had merged to form a separate and distinct personality, that combined the best of each of them. They were so close, he did not know where he ended and Katherine began. Their life together had become so comfortable, he had no idea how to go on without her. He stepped closer to the casket and spoke softly. "Oh, Kate, don't leave me now; not when I need you the most." His tears mixed with the rain running down his face, as he recalled how difficult the trial had been for her. "I promise you, Kate, I will take care of John. We didn't raise him to spend his life in prison, and I will not let that happen. I promise you that." He reached down and touched the casket. "Rest well, my love"

As he turned to leave, Matt was standing behind him with a large brightly colored yellow, green and blue striped golf umbrella. Tom was startled by the umbrellas contrast against the gray sky. He looked at it and smiled. "Your mother would have loved that." Matt held the umbrella over his father and walked him back to the car.

Tom sent his family back to Bay St. Louis, and agreed to meet them there later in the day. He had a stop to make first. John's request to attend his mother's funeral was denied. The headlines, as expected, were sensational, and approving such a request was not the politically correct thing to do.

As John approached his father from behind the glass partition that had become much too familiar to them, the two men studied each other's faces. Tom took his seat. He could see the heartbreak in his son's eyes, and knew he had to set his own grief aside to help John deal with his mother's death.

"She looked beautiful, John, and she knows how you feel. It's all right." John sat down. "She'll never stop loving you. You made her very proud; and she knew this thing is just a big mistake. I told her we are going to take care of it. I promised her that, and we will"

"Dad, I'm so sorry, about everything. Mom would be alive today if it wasn't for me."

"John, that's not true. She was sicker than you know" Tom was prepared for his reaction. "Her heart was very bad. She didn't want you and the others to know. It could have happened at anytime." This was not exactly the truth, but he wanted to relieve John from the guilt he was feeling. John wiped his eyes.

"What are we gonna do now, Dad?"

"What do you mean, what are we going to do now? We're going to get you out of here. That's what we are going to do. I'm going to fire that asshole Hingle, and we'll do this thing right." John's face brightened. "But it's not going to be easy. That's where you come in. You've got three years of law school under your belt, and we need to put that to work. We are going to work side by side day and night. We'll turn this case up side down and shake it until we find what we need to prove you did not kill that girl. Do you understand me?"

"But, how are we going to do that Dad? The sentence is mandatory."

"I'm going to go over all of that with you. What I want you to do now, is get focused and stay strong. I want you to start thinking about this case as a lawyer not as a defendant. You need to get access to law books. I'll handle things outside."

"But Dad that's crazy. What about your job?"

"Forget about the job, Mom and I had good insurance. I don't need a job right now. My job is getting you out of here, but I need you to work with me. Will you do that?"

"Well, yes of course." John managed a smile. "I got plenty of time."

Tom stayed for an hour, reassuring John that together they could do whatever had to be done to overturn the conviction. He asked John to go over the events surrounding the murder to see if anything may have been missed.

"I'll help anyway I can, Dad." John was beginning to share his father's confidence.

"Great. Look I've got to go, now. Got a lot of things to do. Today is Saturday. I'll get back to you as soon as I can; before the end of the week, okay?" He put his palm on the window. John covered it with his own. He could feel his father's strength coming through the glass.

CHAPTER 38

Hingle was preparing to file an appeal. It was a routine response to the conviction. What was not routine was the response he was about to get from Tom Stevens.

Tom did not bother calling for an appointment. He arrived at Hingle's office at 11o'clock Monday morning. Hingle had attended the funeral, but the two men did not speak. Since then Tom thought a lot about the trial and the more he thought about it, the angrier he became.

The receptionist asked if she could help him, but Tom blew by her desk into Hingle's office without a word. He slammed the door; and Hingle, who was looking out the window, jumped about a foot off the floor.

"Tom, I didn't expect you. You should have called." He defensively stepped behind his big leather chair.

"Don't worry, this won't take long. I should have fired your ass after the bail hearing, but I fell for your bullshit, and never realized until it was too late to see what your incompetence was doing to my son. Your defense was pathetic. You handed John to the prosecution on a silver platter. If you knew you couldn't win the case, you should have had the balls to say so. You never tried to defend him against the charges. No, you took the easy way out with that diminished capacity crap. And, only on the last minute, when that wasn't working, you tell the jury, maybe he didn't do it - maybe somebody else did it. Well, it was too late for that. You should have raised that possibility during the trial. You should have challenged the evidence. I ought to throw your fat ass right through that window, you pompous fuck." Hingle cowered behind his chair and braced himself.

"Look, Tom, settle down let me tell you what I'm going to do."

"No, let me tell you what I'm going to do. First I'm going to file a complaint with whoever the hell oversees scum bag lawyers like you. Then, I'm going to appeal the case on the basis of incompetent legal representation. And, if your brilliant legal mind hasn't already figured this out, I am going to find an attorney, who unlike you, can find his legal ass with both hands and who understands the word **defense**, because you are fired." He slammed the door louder on the way out than he did on the way in. Hingle stood frozen behind his chair. No one had ever fired him before.

Tom was not at all sure he had done the right thing, but he felt a lot better, as he sipped a cup of PJ's hazelnut at the Camp Street coffee shop. He had learned a great lesson at John's expense. Against his better judgment and basic instincts, he had allowed Hingle to mislead him and his family into a course of action that defied common sense. Why if they all knew John was innocent, did he not insist on an aggressive defense instead of allowing Hingle to pursue his half-ass **too drunk to know what he was doing strategy?**

One thing that Katherine had said kept echoing in his mind. If John did not kill Mary Simmons, then someone else did. There had to be some evidence that was overlooked. Evidence that the police didn't need and Hingle couldn't find.

Tom ordered another cup of coffee realizing that for the first time in a very long time he had no place to go. With Katherine gone, there was really no one who knew or cared where he was. His family all returned to their jobs after the funeral. They of course all promised to stay in touch, but now, with their mother dead, the distance between them would surely increase, despite their good intentions.

As he finished his second cup, Tom began to realize the commitment he had taken on. His son was sitting in a prison cell under a life sentence, while he was sipping coffee and feeling a little sorry for himself. He had always been self-disciplined when the welfare of his family was concerned. Years of getting out of bed before dawn, and hundreds of thousands of miles on the road chasing sales quotas had never fazed him. He didn't mind the demanding work. He had a mission. He was working to provide his family with what they needed. He was focused.

The task before him now would require nothing less. He needed to fix John's freedom in his mind as his one and only goal, and he needed to develop a plan to achieve that goal. And, he needed to start right now.

The half million dollar insurance settlement did not exactly make him independently wealthy, but it certainly provided him with the opportunity to focus on John's case without financial pressure, at least for a while. He decided to rent an apartment in New Orleans, close to Tulane University, so that he would be closer to John and the crime scene. He also decided to take a couple of courses at Tulane so that he could better understand the basics of criminal law and the legal process.

Finally, he needed another lawyer, and he did not want to make the same mistake in finding one. During the trial there was one man who impressed Tom with his professionalism and knowledge of the law. Perhaps he would be willing to give Tom some direction. He found a phone book and called Judge Patrick Quinton. To his surprise, the Judge agreed to see him, and asked Tom if he could meet him at three o'clock that same day. Tom felt the wheels begin to move. He would certainly be there.

The judge greeted Tom with a warmth that he did not expect. They met in the judge's chambers, surrounded by family photos, sporting trophies and remembrances of people and events that were important to the judge. Respectful of his time, Tom was surprised by Quinton's willingness to engage in pleasant, casual conversation. They were about the same age and both men seemed to have an instant respect for each other. As they chatted about the Saints' terrible season, the big mouth bass hanging on the wall, and anything else that interested them, their mutual respect developed into a comfortable relationship. Without any pressure to do so, Tom eventually lead the conversation around to the purpose of the meeting. He did not dwell on the outcome of the trial, and he leveled no criticism at anyone, but he did make it clear that he wanted his son to have another chance at justice. Judge Quinton did not make Tom ask for his help. He, himself, was not totally comfortable with the outcome of the trial, and he appreciated this father's devotion to his son.

"There is a young lawyer, who works out of the Public Defenders Office. He's very good, knows the law, and is committed to his clients. I think he would be interested in your son's case. You should talk to him. Name is Townsend, Philip Townsend. Tell him I suggested you talk." Quinton scribbled a phone number on a piece of paper and handed it to Tom. He stood and extended his hand to the man he felt he knew better than was possible after the few minutes they had spent together. "Good luck, Tom."

"Thank you, Judge. I appreciate this." The handshake was firm and honest between them. " When I come back to see you, I'll have my son with me."

"I hope you will." The judge walked Tom to the door. "You might be able to catch Townsend on the second floor. Room 214."

The wheels were starting to turn a little faster, now. Tom found Townsend in a corner of the Public Defenders Office buried under an avalanche of file folders. He was about five foot ten, well built, and good looking, with an unruly crop of blonde hair. He looked more like twenty than thirty.

"If Judge Quinton sent you to me, he obviously has no idea of the work load I have here. Gonna have to talk to that man." Townsend stood up and shook Tom's hand, displaying a sense of humor that he had developed from slaying dragons on a daily basis. "I was just thinking about a cup of coffee. Want to join me?"

"Sure, but Mr. Townsend, I don't want to waste your time if you can't help my son."

"Nobody wastes my time. I have no time to waste. Call me Phil, will you? I recognized your name, and I followed your son's case. Let's talk in the cafeteria." Townsend led the way to the room that Tom could now find blindfolded. He and Katherine had spent a lifetime there during the trial.

Townsend listened attentively as Tom related every aspect of the case. He talked about his family, about John, and his law school. He reviewed what had happened during the trial and finally stopped talking with the mention of Katherine's sudden death. Townsend let him catch his breath.

"Mr. Stevens, I do what I do as a PD because our legal system is not always just, especially when a defendant has no high priced counsel like your Mr. Hingle to represent him. I win a lot of cases, not because I am particularly good, but because many times the defendant is innocent, or because he has been denied basic due process. I approach my private practice with the same fundamental principals that I follow as a PD. I work hard to determine the facts, and I argue every case as if it were my only case. There is something about your son's case that does not ring true. I'm not saying that I will be any more successful then my esteemed colleague was, but if you'll allow me, I'd like to review the records, and talk to a few people. After that we can meet again. Fair enough?"

"More than fair." Tom was on his feet. "I want you to know one more thing, Phil. Both John and I are committed to do whatever we can in this effort. I want you to use us in any way you can. I will be available to you day or night."

"Well, that's good to know, Tom. I will need some help with the leg-work and John's education will help me get through the paper work. But, let's not get ahead of ourselves. I'll meet with you again in about a week to see where we are."

"Great, Phil. Thanks for your interest. I'll see you in a week."

It had been a good day. Tom had accomplished much more than he had hoped for. As he walked down the majestic granite steps of the courthouse he decided a steak at Dicky Brennan's was in order. After dinner he would try to call John.

CHAPTER 39

There was a corridor off the gym where the inmates worked out with free weights. John managed to spend a couple of hours in his long week systematically working his muscle groups to counteract the atrophy he felt setting in. After almost seven months he had developed a loose routine, which he tried to follow. He was careful to take care of his own business, and avoid as much contact as possible with other inmates.

The corridor was not well lit, and its slight bend created a blind spot between guard stations. As John worked out, he did not notice that the group of muscle bound morons who usually competed for the weights was unusually small and getting smaller. Before he realized that the only sound around him was coming from his own clanging weights, it was too late. The three gorillas jumped out from behind a locker and landed on top of him. Two held him down with the hundred and fifty pound bar he had been bench pressing. The other one - the one with *Jerome* tattooed on his neck, tore the sweat pants from John's body, and grabbed his genitals with both hands.

"Turn her over gently boys. We don't want to break anything."

They tossed the bar aside as though it was a broomstick. John felt helpless as they lifted his body into the air and flipped him over like a rag doll. While struggling to free himself, he could see Jerome now coming at him, naked from the waste down, and obviously more excited than John wanted to see.

"Spread her out." he said, as the other two grabbed hold of John's legs. "Ain't she pretty?"

As Jerome positioned himself between John's legs, John jerked his right leg free, and managed to deliver a direct hit to the enormous set of balls that was approaching him. Jerome dropped to the floor in excruciating pain. Instinctively, the others let go of John to attend to their friend. John moved quickly, picking up a ten-pound iron disk, and slamming it up against the first head within range. Blood gushed from the side of the head, and another of John's suitors fell to the floor, howling in pain.

John reached for another weight, but before he could use it, he felt a stinging, right cross that lifted him off the floor and sent him reeling across the room. Slumped over like a sack of rice against the wall, he could see the last two hundred and sixty pound Neanderthal coming after him. As John regained his footing, the only thing between him and his attacker was a lifting bench with an empty steel bar resting in the cradle. Drawing as much inner strength as he could, John shoved the bar toward his target. The steel bar flew out of the cradle and delivered a crushing blow right above his attacker's heart. It stopped him cold. As he grabbed his chest, his knees buckled under him. Instinctively, John caught the rebounding bar in his arms, and swung it at his assailant's head. It was a home run. The man's eyes rolled back, as he fell face first, smashing his nose on the concrete floor.

John spun around quickly like a Samaria warrior to ward off another attacker, but there were no more. Only Jerome was moving, still rolling on the floor in agony. In disbelief, John looked around at his handy work, and carefully positioned the bar back in the cradle. He quickly pulled on his sweat pants and quietly left the area, trying his best to act like nothing had happened.

It wasn't until the next morning at breakfast when he realized the full extent of the damage. John braced for another attack as Jerome approached him carrying a steel tray. His two accomplices followed him, both looking like Q-tips, with their entire heads wrapped tight with cotton and gauze. John stood his ground. When their eyes met, Jerome adjusted his aching balls in his jockey shorts and quickly turned away. The Q-tips followed their leader to a table far away from John.

By the end of the day John had become a legend in his own time, winning instant VIP status, reserved only for those who were not to be messed with. Fortunately for John, nothing was reported, and nothing more came from the incident, except that it was exactly what he needed in order to be left alone.

CHAPTER 40

By Wednesday Phil Townsend had decided to take the case. He had already collected the files from Hingle's office and he'd begun to review the evidence. He scrutinized the crime scene photographs, and studied the forensic records. There had to be something there - something that might cast some doubt about his new client's guilt. Unfortunately, because Hingle had speculated to John's fingerprints being on the knife, there was little in the trial transcript relating to forensic testimony. He had to rely on the written reports. His biggest problem was the knife. There was no doubt that the prints were John's, but if he didn't kill the girl, how did they get on the knife? That's what he needed to know.

On Thursday, he called Tom and asked him to meet him at the Police station. Tom was there in a half hour. Townsend was well known to the New Orleans Police. Even though he had made them look foolish on several occasions, the police respected him as a good attorney. He casually introduced Tom as an associate who would be working with him on an appeal case. When he asked to view the physical evidence from the Simmon's murder case, they were directed, without question to the evidence room, where several boxes of miscellaneous items were made available to them.

Phil dug through the boxes containing beer cans and ashtrays, and pieces of blood soaked clothing. Finally he found the plastic bag he was looking for. It contained the murder weapon. Tom was already feeling a little queasy about this collection of death scene memorabilia, but the sight of the knife, close up, made him take a step back. He didn't realize it was so big. It was the largest in a set of fine steel carving knives, designed with a pistol grip to provide a secure and comfortable handle. Phil examined the knife closely while reading the forensic report's specific details about the prints. The complete palm print identified in the report was still clearly visible in dried blood on the knife handle.

Townsend then flipped through the pictures of the dead women, taken from every imaginable angle. He selected about six pictures and arranged them on the table.

"Pass me that coroner's report, will you, Tom?" Phil pointed to an envelope that he had brought along. Tom obliged, having no idea at all what was going on.

"You see something, Phil?"

"Oh, I don't know, maybe." Phil skimmed through the report and stopped at the section that dealt with the cause of death. The coroner stated that the victim was killed by a fatal stab wound that entered below her collarbone and over her right breast. The blade plunged through the lung and into the heart, causing instant death. There were many other stab wounds, some more serious than others, but this was the injury that actually caused her death, according to the report. "This one here." Phil said pointing to one of the photographs. "This clearly shows the wound that killed her." He took a magnifying glass from his brief case and examined the picture closely. He then turned back quickly to the coroner's report. Within the text was a front and back sketch of a body, indicating the location of the wounds. He turned to another section that described the fatal wound and read out loud.

The wound measures two and one half inches in length. It is wedge shaped, slightly wider at the bottom than the top.

He stopped reading and squinted as though his mind were trying to visualize something.

"Got something?" Tom was fascinated.

"I think so, Tom. Let's get out of here. We need to go shopping." He copied the brand name from the knife blade.

"Shopping for what?"

" We're gonna buy a knife."

"A knife. Okay, whatever you say, you're the boss."

They found what they were looking for at a specialty shop in the mall next to the Superdome. It was an exact duplicate of the murder weapon. Tom had to buy the whole set of six knives to get the one Phil needed, but he was happy to hand over the eighty dollars.

Phil had also called the landlord earlier in the day to make arrangements to visit the crime scene. At about four o'clock both he and Tom found themselves standing in the kitchen of John's former apartment on the exact spot where Mary Simmons's body was found. Tom had listened carefully at the trial as each of the witnesses talked about being in the apartment, but seeing the actual apartment and its furnishings made the murder so much more real to him. He stepped out of the kitchen into the bathroom and tried to visualize John lying in the bathtub. He took note of the porcelain soap dish, that John's head hit as he fell.

"Tom, come over here will you?" Phil was standing in the kitchen holding the shinny new knife. Tom approached him carefully.

"What are you going to do, Phil?"

Phil turned Tom so the two men were facing each other.

"You're a little taller than me, so I will be the victim. The coroner says the fatal wound was inflicted below the collarbone and over the right breast. I want you to take the knife and proceed as you would to inflict the fatal blow."

"You mean like this?" Tom raised the knife above his head and slowly brought it down to the pre-determined point of entry.

"Exactly, now do that again." Phil watched as Tom repeated the movement. "One more time, slowly. Notice anything?"

"Not especially." Tom continued the motion. "What am I missing?"

"Look at how you are holding the knife." Phil took Tom by the wrist and lowered the knife. "It's upside down with the pistol grip pointing up."

The knife was indeed upside down. Tom had gripped the knife in the way that felt most comfortable to him, without any thought of its position.

"You're right. It is, but that's just the way I picked it up. What does it mean?"

"It means that you handled the knife exactly the way the killer did, which is the most comfortable and natural way to hold it above your head if you were delivering a downward blow."

"But, how do you know the killer held the knife in the same way?"

"You remember the coroners report?" Townsend picked up the file. "The coroner said the fatal wound was wedge shaped, wider at the bottom than the top." Before he could finish, Tom interrupted him.

"Which means that the blade entered the body upside down."

"Exactly, but that's not the good part." He opened his brief case and took out a photograph of the murder weapon and a copy of the forensic report. "The good part is here." He read from the report, while handing Tom the picture that clearly showed the dried palm print around the knife handle.

The weapon clearly displays a full palm print on the right side of the wooden handle and corresponding fingerprints on the left side of the handle.

Tom looked again at the knife in his hand, and studied it for a moment before the light bulb went on. "My palm is on the left side of the handle, not the right. If I turn the knife so that my palm is on the right side, there's no way I could make that particular wound with the blade upside down."

"That's right, and that means that because John's right hand palm print is on the right side of the handle, there is no way that he could have inflicted the fatal wound either."

"But, wait a minute, what does this mean?" Tom's brain was not working quite as fast as Phil's.

"It can only mean that the killer put the bloody knife in John's hand while he was unconscious, in order to imprint his palm and fingers on the handle and to incriminate him. But the killer made a big mistake. He put the knife in John's hand as though he were going to carve a turkey, pistol grip down, palm on the right side. If John raised the knife above his head while holding it like that, the blade would be pointing backwards, with the handle facing the victim."

Tom turned the knife in his hand so as to mimic the bloody print on the murder weapon. Raising it above his head, he repeated the earlier stabbing movement, bringing the butt of the handle down slowly to the fatal spot above Phil's right breast.

"Well I'll be god-damned."

CHAPTER 41

It was Friday, three in the morning. Fred Roberts woke from a sound sleep with one word burning in his brain, *Rabbinni*. He sat up straight in bed trying to clear his head. When he first read that name in his daughter's calendar, it sounded familiar, but he was unable to make a connection. He hadn't thought about it for several weeks, but now at three in the morning, while he slept, his subconscious mind had solved the puzzle. Rabbinni was the name of the guy who killed his daughter. Detective Crawford told him that name. He was sure of it. The revelation was startling. Did Courtney know the man who killed her? Was it a coincidence that she had some business with him while in school? The connection troubled him. Unable to sleep, he went to his study and opened Courtney' s secretary, and began reading the calendar entries. There it was.

March 20,1998, 10:00 AM Law Clinic

Meet with Mary regarding Rabbinni.

He flipped through the remaining pages and found the name Rabbinni four more times.

The last entry was on April 29, 1998.

Review Rabbinni with Mary and advisor.

Was it possible that this Rabbinni was not Crawford's Rabbinni? How many Rabbinnis could there be? Fred did not like the smell of this coincidence, and in spite of the early hour, he decided to try to reach Detective Crawford.

Crawford was not at the station and was not expected until eight o'clock. Fred could not wait and decided to try him at the private number Crawford had given him

"This better be good." Crawford answered with a voice that had just been awakened from a deep sleep. He slept alone since losing his wife to cancer two years earlier.

"Detective Crawford, this is Fred Roberts. I hate to call you this early but I have something that I have to talk to you about." There was silence on the other end, and Fred thought for a moment that the connection was broken. "Are you there?"

"Yes, I'm here. Who did you say this was?" Crawford was now sitting on the edge of his bed.

"Fred Roberts. You handled my daughter's case. The hit and run?"

"Oh yes, yes, Mr. Roberts, I'm afraid, I'm not too sharp at this time of the morning. What can I do for you?"

"Well, I'd like to get together with you if we could. I've got something that I think you should see."

"O'kay, that's fine. How bout we meet for coffee at about seven? Where are you now?"

"I'm in Daytona, but I can be in your office by seven."

"Daytona? Must be pretty important. You got about a three-hour drive." Crawford's interest was peaking.

"I think it is very important. I'll be there by seven."

"That's Good, because I got something to tell you also. I'll wait till I see you."

Fred showered, and after a quick coffee was on his way to Mississippi. As he drove through the early morning darkness he thought about the entries he had read. Each one that mentioned Rabbinni also mentioned Mary. Mary who? Do to his business travels Fred had not met many of Courtney's acquaintances. Maybe Crawford could locate this Mary and find out what Courtney's connection to Rabbinni was.

He pulled into the parking lot at the Mississippi State Police Headquarters at ten minutes to seven. Crawford was outside waiting for him.

"Good morning. You made good time." Crawford showed no signs of being upset about the early wakeup call.

"Yes, very little traffic this time of the morning." Fred collected his daughter's leather secretary from the passenger seat of his Lexus, and stepped out.

"I thought we'd go down the road to a little truck stop where we can talk away from the phones. That sound okay to you?" Crawford opened the passenger door to his unmarked LTD cruiser.

"Sounds fine. Did you say you had something to tell me?" Fred remembered the early conversation.

"Yes, it's strange that you called when you did." Crawford pulled out of the parking lot and headed west. "I would have called you if you had-n't. It seems our friend Rabbinni has escaped."

"Escaped, what do you mean escaped? How can that happen?" Fred was startled by the news in light of what he had discovered.

"Not sure yet. Lot of unanswered questions. He was being transported from the prison to the hospital when the vehicle he was in was overtaken on the highway. Two guards were killed and Rabbinni escaped with a little help from his friends. I told you there was more to this guy than we thought." Crawford pulled off the road and parked next to a sixteen wheeler.

"Well, then I think you will really be interested in what I have to show you."

Fred was right. As the two men sipped coffee, Crawford turned the pages of the secretary.

"God Damn. This is no coincidence. Your daughter knew this guy. Met with him on several occasions according to this."

"I know. That's why I wanted to get this to you." Fred felt good that Crawford had verified the importance of his discovery. " What are you going to do?"

"You don't mind if I hang on this do you?"

"No, but I'd like to get it back sometime."

"Oh, sure don't worry about that." Crawford was copying names and addresses from the binder. "What I'm gonna do is, I'm gonna try to find some of these people in your daughter's book here. I know a little bit about this Tulane Law Clinic that Rabbinni and your daughter apparently had some connection with. The clinic gets involved in a lot of environmental issues. The law students sue big businesses on behalf of the little guy. I remember reading that the Tulane students had become a real pain in the ass to some big refinery in Louisiana. It became a big political hot potato. Maybe there's some connection there. Anyway, with Rabbinni on the loose this may be as good a place as any to start looking for him."

"So, what? This guy is wanted for murder now?" Fred was referring to the apparent escape.

"Looks like it. We're not sure who did the shooting. But, listen I'm glad you called. This could be very important in helping us find him. We will also want to question him more about your daughter's death. That sure don't look like no accident now."

The two men finished their coffee and returned to the police station. Crawford shook Fred's hand and thanked him again. As Fred headed back to Florida he was sure he had done the right thing.

CHAPTER 42

On Friday evening, Tom drove back to Bay St Louis. Being away for a few days, he wanted to check on the house and pick up a few things for the apartment in New Orleans. As he emptied the mailbox in front of the house, a small brown box fell from the assortment of magazines, bills and letters. As he picked it up, he saw that it was addressed to John. He held the mail under his chin while he fumbled around with the key to the front door. As luck would have it, he could hear the phone ringing in the house. Finally, the right key clicked the door open. Tom threw the mail on the table and lunged for the phone.

"Hello, this is Tom."

"Dad, this is John. I 'm glad I caught you. I was just going to hang up."

"John, you wouldn't believe it. I just walked in the door. I've been in New Orleans all week. I was going to call you tonight. Got a lot of news."

"Me too Dad. I wanted to tell you I got access to the library here. They've got a good collection of law books, and I've been able to research a number of cases already." John was sounding more upbeat than he had been in along time.

191

"John, wait until I tell you what Phil Townsend has come up with already." The father and son talked for an hour. Tom filled John in on the knife discovery, and John almost came through the phone when he realized the importance of the news.

"Jesus, that's great, Dad. That means I could not have killed Mary. I knew it. So what's the next step? How is Townsend going to use the information?"

"I'm not sure how he plans to appeal." Tom explained that on the basis of his discovery Townsend might try to demonstrate that John did not inflict the fatal blow, or at least establish that the forensic evidence was not properly considered by the previous defense attorney. He told John that Phil was sure the appeal would be granted, but that Phil needed to do a lot more work to prepare for it.

"John, Phil will be coming to see you very soon. He wants to go over the whole story again. Have you been able to recall anything else? He's going to need all the help you can give him."

"No not really, but I'm working on it. I am also putting together a list of people who Mary had contact with, to see if there might be someone who she had a problem with." John was enthusiastic about this new mission.

"That's good, John. That's the kind of thing you need to be doing. I'm sure Phil will agree." Tom was now sorting the mail on the table while he talked. " By the way I have a package here for you."

"A package?" John sounded puzzled. "What kind of package?"

"I don't know it's very small. Do you want me to open it?"

"Sure, Dad, go ahead. You got me curious."

Tom removed the wrapper and opened the box. "It's a ring. A very beautiful ring."

"Oh God, that must be Mary's ring. How did you get it?"

"I don't really know. It came in the mail." Tom examined the ring. It was a one caret VSI diamond in a solitaire white gold setting. "You must have given a good dollar for this."

"Yes, four thousand dollars. I charged it. I wanted to surprise her after graduation. Courtney was holding it for me. She must have mailed it before the accident."

"I don't think so." Tom looked at the postmark. "It was mailed from Florida just a few days ago. There is a short note with it." Tom read the note. "John, good luck to you and Mary. You're perfect for each other. Call me in Florida. Love Courtney. And there's a phone number."

"Wow, I didn't think I'd ever see that ring again. Maybe Courtney's father sent it to me. Would you do me a favor, Dad, and call Mr. Roberts, and thank him for me." I don't want to call him from here."

"Sure, Son, I'll call him, as soon as we hang up." The two talked for another ten minutes, before saying goodbye. They decided to turn the ring over to Phil Townsend. He may be able to use it to prove how John really felt about Mary.

Tom made himself a cup of coffee, and dialed the number on the note.

"Hello." Fred Roberts answered. It had been a long day and he was tired from driving.

"Hello, Mr. Roberts, My name is Tom Stevens."

"Yes." Fred did not recognize the name.

"I'm John Stevens father. I think you just mailed a package to him."

"Oh yes, Tom, I'm glad he got it. I found it among my daughter belongings. Was it important?"

"Yes it's very important to John, and he wanted me to call you and express his thanks." Tom then proceeded to give Fred a little background on what had happened. "So, Courtney and Mary and John were apparently all very good friends, and it's incredible to think about the tragedy that has fallen on all three families." Fred had not followed the trial, and the names of Mary Simmons and John Stevens did not mean much to him, but Fred did remember that Courtney repeatedly referred to a Mary when she wrote about Rabbinni. He decided to confide in Tom and fill him in on what he and Detective Crawford had talked about.

"So, you see, this guy Abdul Rabbinni, who killed my daughter and Allison McKay, has also killed two police officers, and he is now on the loose; and it is very possible that the Mary referred to in Courtney's journal is this Mary Simmons, who you say was murdered. This is very strange."

"Stranger than hair on a cue ball." Tom said to himself. "Fred do you have anything that might tell us what involvement your daughter had with this Rabbinni guy?"

"I don't know. I have a lot of Courtney's notebooks and things but I haven't really gone through them. All I can really tell you is when Courtney mentioned Rabbinni and Mary in her calendar, it was always in relation to the Tulane Law Clinic."

Tom remembered some talk about Mary being involved with the Law Clinic at school. He would ask John more about it when they talked again. In the meantime, he thought Phil Townsend might be interested in knowing about this link between the two dead girls.

CHAPTER 43

Don Crawford was already in New Orleans. After talking with Fred Roberts, he thought he might get a lead on the location of Abdul Rabbinni by talking to someone at the Law Clinic. His appointment was with Professor Norman Norton who was the Law Clinic coordinator. Norton was a short man with a bow tie. He was balding, but tried to hide it by combing what little hair he had from over his left ear across the top of his head. As Crawford thought how silly the hair looked, he asked Norton if he had any knowledge of Rabbinni. Norton's expression suddenly changed. It was clear that he had indeed.

"That fruit cake drove us crazy." Norton approached the file cabinet in the office.

"What do you mean?" Crawford remembered the day he had arrested Rabbinni in the toilet stall.

"He was an asylum case. Had a long tale of woe about being persecuted in Afghanistan by the Taliban. Said he faced certain death if he was returned to his country. The Law Clinic represents people who are legitimately seeking asylum for fear of persecution in their homeland. But this guy was a pain in the ass to the student assigned to his case."

"How so?" The detective did not divulge that he knew about Courtney Roberts.

"Well, he had a very convincing story about being forced into service by the Taliban army with other young men from his village, only to die on the front line. It seems the Taliban would force the Afghanistans to perform the most hazardous combat assignments. Instead of joining the army and facing certain death, he hid in the chassis of a truck that carried him over the border to Pakistan, where he lived under cover for a year. According to his story, he made some Pakistani friends who eventually helped him stowaway on a ship heading for America."

"So, what about the students?"

"He drove them nuts, calling them at all times of the day and night. Insisting that they meet with him all the time. Demanding that they work harder on his case, and ultimately berating them when the judge finally denied his asylum application." Crawford put his hand out to accept the files that Norton had taken from the drawer.

"Can you tell me about the students who were assigned to the case?"

"Two of our best. Very bright girls committed to their clients, Courtney Roberts and Mary Ellen Simmons. They were good friends and liked to work together. They had won a couple of cases, but this one was a nightmare for them. They both tried to get out of the case; but he would not let them. Unfortunately, both girls have since met with tragic and untimely deaths."

"Both girls?" Detective Crawford looked up from the files.

"Yes Courtney was killed in a hit and run automobile accident; and Mary Simmons was murdered by a jealous boyfriend. Tragic. Both of them. The whole university was in shock."

"I'm sure." Crawford had found the mysterious Mary and another strange coincidence. "Listen would it be possible for me to stay here and look through these files for a while."

"Well, we close at three, and its ten minutes 'til, but, if this is official police business, you're welcome to sign them out." Norton turned a register toward Crawford and handed him a pen. "I don't think anyone will be looking for them."

Crawford signed his name and left with the files. He called his office advising his captain that he was spending the night in New Orleans, so that he would not waste time driving back to Mississippi. He crossed over the Mississippi River Bridge to the New Orleans West Bank were he knew he could get a cheap room at the Holiday Inn under the southwest expressway. After a quick meal at Applebee's on General DeGaule Drive, he returned to the Motel to read through the files.

They were neatly arranged, beginning with a comprehensive history of the applicant. There were extensive notes, entered by both Mary Simmons and Courtney Roberts, covering in detail the progression of the case through to the final hearing before the Judge. Crawford tried to correlate the meeting dates on Courtney's calendar with the notes in the files. Under *Meeting Minutes*, he found a file for the April 29th meeting with the advisor.

The minutes related to a conversation held between Mary and Courtney and the faculty advisor who was assisting them with the Rabbinni case. The girls clearly stated the difficulty that they were both experiencing with Mr. Rabbinni. At first he would send them expensive gifts, and refuse to take them back when the girls insisted. He would then show up unannounced between classes and monopolize their time with questions about the status of his case. He was unreasonably impatient with the legal process, calling late at night to demand that the girls call the judge to move his case along. He would break out in a rage when he felt the girls were not working hard enough. Mary wrote that only after trying to reason with Mr. Rabbinni unsuccessfully, were they turning to the advisor for some help. In her final sentence she wrote:

I do not believe Mr. Rabbinni is stable. He has made it clear to Courtney and I that he is holding us personally responsible for the outcome of his hearing. I fear that if he is not allowed to stay in the U.S., we may be in danger.

Crawford stared at the sentence, paying little attention to the knock on his door.

"Towels, Mr. Crawford." He got up from the desk, and walked to the door as he continued to read.

"Okay, thanks." He threw the latch and opened the door. "But, I really don't need any more towels"

The gunshots sounded like they were fired under water. The two small holes in Don Crawford's face, one under the left eye and one in the middle of his forehead, first looked like spots of ink that could be wiped away. He stood staring at his assailant unable to move. Then the blood began running down his face, and he fell back across the bed. Within moments he was dead. The assailant stepped into the room and collected the files that were spread across the desk. Seconds later he was gone.

CHAPTER 44

"Fred, this is Tom Stevens. Have you heard the news?" The Saturday noon news cast reported the shooting death of the Mississippi state trooper in a West bank Motel. The trooper had been identified, but no more details of the shooting were being released.

"Hi, Tom, what news?"

"Detective Crawford's been shot. He's dead."

"What? You have got to be kidding." Fred immediately regretted not having a more intelligent response. "I mean - I just talked with him. How could that happen? Christ did it have anything to do with Rabbinni?"

"I don't know, Fred. I'm waiting for the next bulletin. Do you know what he was doing in New Orleans?"

"I'm not sure, but he said he was going to the Tulane Law Clinic to see if he could get a lead on Rabbinni's whereabouts."

"Jesus, that doesn't sound good. Tom had not been able to reach Phil Townsend since Friday night when he told him about his earlier conversation with Fred. Things were happening so fast. "Listen were you able to find anything in your daughters belongings about Rabbinni."

"No, Tom. I went through everything. The only thing I had was her journal, and I gave that to Crawford." He apologized.

"That's alright, Fred. If you do come across anything will you call me?"

"Sure. Let me know what they say about Crawford will you? I don't get the New Orleans news here."

When the two hung up, Tom tried Townsend's home number again. He had already left a message for Phil and did not bother repeating it. He left his apartment and headed for St. Charles Avenue.

Mighty oak trees twisted and knurled from centuries of pruning formed a protective canopy over the neutral ground where the streetcars traveled up and down St. Charles Avenue. This was New Orleans's most prestigious neighborhood. Historic Victorian mansions, built hundreds of years ago by industrialists, lined the avenue. Behind them, shielded from view, were rows of modest houses, built to quarter the black folks who toiled in the mansions during the days of slavery. Today these structures have all been renovated; and they command extremely high prices in a very exclusive real estate market. Tulane University occupies a number of prominent buildings amid the grand mansions across from Audubon Park.

Tom was not sure where he was going as he drove along the avenue, but he needed to know if Detective Crawford had visited the campus as Fred said he intended to. He eventually found his way to the Law Clinic, and was greeted by a very distraught Professor Norton.

"I am very sorry." He said. "But something very terrible happened here yesterday, and I am very upset about it." He was obviously flustered as he nervously moved files from one cabinet to another for no apparent reason.

"Did it involve Detective Crawford?" Tom assumed it did.

"Oh my God, yes." Norton, startled, spun around quickly to face Tom, dislocating the ten-inch flap of hair, which he had meticulously pasted over the top of his bald head. The hair now hung down over his ear, completely exposing his shiny scalp. "Who are you?"

"I'm Tom Stevens. I am working with attorney Philip Townsend." Tom tried not to look at the hair until Norton had it pulled back in place. "I would like to know if you talked with Detective Crawford yesterday."

"Yes, I talked with him, and he took the files." Norton was shaken. "And now he's dead. Shot to death."

"Can you tell me what you talked about - what files you gave him?"

"Oh this is very upsetting. I'm not sure if I should talk to you or anybody. Are the police coming to see me?" The hair was not quite right yet.

"I don't know about that, professor." Tom tried to calm him. "I just need to know what you talked about, and what was in those files that the detective took."

"It was about those girls and that fruitcake Rabbinni. He took the Rabbinni file."

"What girls are you talking about?"

"Courtney Roberts and Mary Simmons. They're both dead. They worked on the Rabbinni case together, and now the whole file is gone and detective Crawford, who took it, is dead as well."

"Do you know what was in that file?" With Mary Simmons now definitely tied to Rabbinni, Tom knew that he had stumbled on to something that may be important to his son's case.

"I know generally what's in it. I was their advisor, but I can't say I know everything. It contained the girls' notes and a history of the case. It's the only copy we have. I told the detective that Mr. Rabbinni was a very difficult man who made those girls miserable. He even threatened them."

Tom wanted desperately to talk to Phil Townsend. He thanked the professor and set out to find him. As he left the office the receptionist was watching a TV news bulletin. The small screen was filled with a headshot of an Afghanistan national, as a reporter read the news.

"The FBI has released this photo of Abdul Rabbinni wanted in connection with the killing of two police officers in Mississippi last week during a successful break from federal prison. An FBI representative warns that Rabbinni is armed and extremely dangerous. He is part of a well-organized group of Islamic terrorists, sworn to over throw the United States from within its own boundaries. Police report that Rabbinni and his accomplices are committed to taking American lives, and will stop at nothing to accomplish their objectives."

The report went on to say that Rabbinni was thought to be operating along the gulf cost from Florida to Louisiana.

"Oh, my God." Professor Norton also heard the newscast from his office.

Less than two miles away, on the second floor of a rundown building in the warehouse district off Tchopotoulas Street, Abdul Rabbinni and two other Iranian zealots sat on crates filled with explosives and automatic weapons. Over a small fire in an empty trashcan, Rabbinni was carefully burning each page of the file he had taken from Detective Crawford. Behind him, tacked on a wall, was a floor plan of the Morial Convention Center. The building itself, which was built in three phases and covered more than a million square feet, could be seen from the open warehouse window. It was December 10th, less than three weeks until the start of the festival season, which would last until Fat Tuesday —Mardi Gras.

CHAPTER 45

Tom did not find Phil Townsend. Townsend found him. He was waiting for Tom when Tom arrived at his new apartment.

"Phil, I've been trying to reach you all day." Tom said as he stepped out of his car.

"Been busy, Tom." Phil stepped off the porch and extended his hand. "Went up to see John. He's doing fine."

"Oh, did you? That's great. I told him you would be up to talk to him." Tom unlocked the right side of the duplex and invited Phil into his four-room apartment. "Are you aware of what's been going on, Phil?"

"You mean that apparently Mary Simmons had some connection with this Rabbinni character, who is the same guy who killed Courtney Roberts and Allison McKay, and two cops in Mississippi, and probably detective Crawford as well; and who I think we will find also killed the Simmons girl?"

"Yes, yes, can you believe it?" Tom opened the refrigerator and opened two Bud long necks. I went to Tulane, and talked to a Professor Norton. He wasn't very helpful, but he did confirm that Crawford was there and that he took the Rabbinni file with him."

"I know, I talked with Norton, after you did." Phil enjoyed a long swallow of the cold beer as he took a seat at the kitchen table. "I also talked with the Feds who are tracking Rabbinni. They want this guy and his friends very badly. They were not aware of his link to the girls"

"Do you really think this guy killed those girls like that?"

"I can't say for sure, but I do know that Rabbinni and fanatics like him don't think like you and I. Norton said he was enraged when his asylum was denied. He took it as a personal insult and threatened to get even. Everyone thought he was a nut, and no one took him seriously. The McKay girl was in the wrong place at the wrong time, but I think the other two were clearly revenge murders. He believed they did him wrong, and he got even."

"What about Crawford?" Tom could not believe how fast Phil's mind worked.

"Crawford arrested Rabbinni initially. Rabbinni probably planned to kill him also, and was looking for the opportunity when Crawford started getting close to the other murders."

"So that's it then." Tom opened another beer. "Rabbinni killed Mary Simmons and planted the knife on John. How do we get John out of prison?" he handed another beer to Townsend.

"Wait a minute, Tom. We got a pretty good theory here, but without any proof, that's all we have. And, Rabbinni and his cohorts could be back in Iran by now for all we know. With that file gone, we have no tangible evidence that connects Rabbinni to the girls."

"But there are witnesses. Can't we get Norton to tell the judge that Rabbinni was threatening the girls?"

"We can; but his testimony would be hearsay, with no documentation to support it. If we could find that file, I think we would have what we need to make a very strong appeal."

Tom considered Townsend' s astute observation. Of course he was right, but still Tom was encouraged. They were a hell of a lot closer to freeing John than they were a week earlier.

"What about John, Phil. You said he was doing well?"

"Yes his spirits are up. He is very enthusiastic about what you are doing for him? I went over the case with him. He is very believable. He really does not remember anything, but he is greatly relieved to know that he did not kill his girlfriend."

"Did you ask him about Mary and Rabbinni? Maybe she told him about this asshole."

"I thought of that. He seems to recall Mary telling him about being assigned the case, but she did not talk about it much after that. She no doubt respected the confidentiality."

"So where does that leave us? What do we do now?" Tom was beginning to get restless.

Phil finished his beer and got up from the table.

"Well, I got John working on a brief. He will be helping me put the appeal together. I am going to meet with the locals tomorrow to see what they have come up with regarding the Crawford murder. That file may have turned up."

"Good, I'll go with you."

"No, what I'd like you to do, Tom, is to go back and see Professor Norton again in the morning. See if you can get him to relax and talk to you. If he was the advisor on the Rabbinni case, he must have some records or references that we may be able to use. I'd like you to get a complete statement from him also if you can. Maybe he can recall something else that will physically connect Rabbinni to the dead girls." Tom was more than happy to take the assignment, although the idea of trying to interview Norton while looking at that hair brought a smile to his face. "One more thing, Tom. Remember these people may still be around, and they are very dangerous. Be very careful. I mean that."

It had never occurred to Tom that he was involved in an active murder investigation, and the murderer or murderers may be a threat to him. But, Phil was right the body count was beginning to add up, and with the savage way that Rabbinni killed, he would not hesitate to eliminate anyone who got in his way.

"Okay, Phil, I will." He walked Townsend to the front door and promised to report to him as soon as he talked to Norton.

It was 4:30 PM. The Law clinic was closed, but Professor Norton was busy in his office rearranging files, and trying to keep his mind off the events of the previous two days. First there was the detective, who got shot. Then there was the guy who worked for the attorney, and then the attorney himself. And after he left, the FBI came calling. Norton was not the type to be involved in any kind of controversy. He liked to keep to himself and do his work. But during the last few days, he had more visitors than he'd seen in the last year, and all the disruption had irritated his stomach ulcer. He decided to get his office reorganized and take a vacation.

He did not hear the click of the lock on the front door. The receptionist had left at four, and there was no one to warn him of the intruder, who had skillfully foiled the lock. Norton continued to sort though his file cabinets when the figure appeared in the corner of his eye. He turned quickly in time to say only one word. "You." The blade appeared from out of nowhere and slashed through the professor's neck like warm butter. He grabbed his throat as his windpipe clamped shut. The blood started slowly, but soon flowed freely through his fingers and down the front of his starched white shirt. His knees hit the floor first, and then he fell forward against the file cabinet. Rabbinni was gone before the professor's heart stopped.

CHAPTER 46

It was a new idea and promised to be a bigger celebration than all other Mardi Gras events. Bacchus, Zulu, Endymion, and scores of other krewes all planned their traditional elaborate balls and enormous parades. Each one would fill the streets of New Orleans with millions of spectators from New Years Day to Fat Tuesday. Three billion dollars would be pumped into the local economy during the two-month long carnival season.

But, as awesome as each separate event would be, none could compete with the **Ball of Kings.** After years of negotiating among all of the various krewes who held fast to their own sacred and secret traditions, an agreement had been finally reached to bring all of the krewes together for one mega event. The historic first **Ball of Kings** would be held at the Morial Convention Center on the first Sunday after New Years Day, January 3, 1999. The theme was to pay tribute to all the past kings from all the various krewes who had served throughout the colorful history of Mardi Gras. It was being hailed as an international event. Celebrities from all over the world would converge on the Convention Center and join with tens of thousands of revelers who would get lost in the madness of the world's greatest party town.

There would be the traditional formal, tongue in cheek, pomp and ceremony, in the historic Mardi Gras style. But, this year the honorary kings would not only pay homage to themselves, but they would also welcome the President of the United States as well as political leaders from all over the free world.

Security would, of course, be of the highest level, and for months ahead of the scheduled event, security forces had been carefully positioning themselves to monitor unusual traffic in and out of New Orleans. Any new activity, or events out of the ordinary were being closely scrutinized. By the time the **Ball of Kings** arrived, New Orleans would be like a fortress protected from any outside forces that would disrupt or threaten the celebration.

Abdul Rabbinni was not concerned about security. His organization had been aware of the pending **Ball of King's** for over a year, and since then, little by little he had been positioning his followers all over New Orleans in legitimate jobs, many relating to the operations of the Convention Center. They were in food service, transportation, maintenance, entertainment, emergency medical and even security positions - all working with proper credentials for legitimate companies.

Indeed the very warehouse where they had set up a headquarters was within a quarter mile of the Convention Center, and it was owned by a legitimate U.S. company controlled by Rabbinni's sympathizers. Freight moved in and out of the warehouse every day, and the munitions stored on the second floor - enough to level half the city- appeared no more unusual than the other machinery, and equipment being forwarded to businesses every day all over New Orleans. Everything was already in place, and the plan to destroy the Convention Center and everyone near it during the **Ball of Kings** could be activated within an hour's time.

There had been only one small problem. His organization had been successful in using many resources to bring his followers into the

United States. One of the most effective was the Law Clinic at Tulane University. During the last several years, bright, young, hardworking, but somewhat naive law students, were successful in gaining asylum for twelve of Rabbinni's most loyal followers. He had not anticipated the problem that he, himself, had encountered. It was his plan to enter the country legally by being granted asylum, so that he could carry out his mission with as little difficulty and interference as possible. The denial of his petition enraged him. The continuous disrespect shown to him by the female student lawyers assigned to his case was an insult, which he swore to avenge.

Rabbinni had stalked Mary Simmons for days and was outside John Steven's apartment on the night of the party. He followed Mary back into the apartment after she said good night to Courtney Roberts and Allison McKay. Mary would have gone home also, if she had not forgotten her car keys in the apartment.

He silently entered the apartment right behind her, and removed a kitchen knife from its holder on the kitchen counter, while Mary checked on John. Not seeing him in bed, she was startled to find that he had fallen into the tub and knocked himself out. When she returned to the kitchen to call for help, Rabbinni lunged at her and began his savage assault. He continued slashing until his anger had subsided. Then in his final twisted act of revenge, he cleaned the knife of his own prints, dipped it in Mary's blood and pressed it into John's hand. He was very careful to leave no evidence of his ever being there.

Courtney Robert's killing did not go as well. His capture had been unfortunate. But it was over now, and the injustice had been avenged. He had eliminated some other bothersome details, and his attention was again focused on the sensational attack that would bring him honor and glory in his homeland. He had only two weeks to wait.

Across town, Tom poured himself a cup of coffee, and opened the Times Picayune. He could not move the cup to his mouth as he starred at the headline:

BRUTAL SLAYING OF PROFESSOR SHOCKS TULANE COMMUNITY

"Rabbinni," He said. "he's still here in the city." He lowered the coffee cup slowly to the table. Had this maniac actually killed again? Tom read the article turning quickly to page three. As he finished, he dialed Phil's number. It rang once before he picked up.

"Phil Townsend."

"Have you seen the paper?"

"Tom," He recognized Tom's excited voice. "Yes I have. Must have happened last night after we talked. The secretary found him this morning. I guess you won't be doing that interview today." Tom was not seasoned enough to be able to make light of such violence, nor did he know that those who must deal with it every day often resort to humor to help them cope.

"I guess not, but I'm beginning to feel like this guy is living with me."

"Well, he is covering his tracks very well. Norton was the last one who knew about his threats to the murdered girls. Without him and that file we got nothing to support our theory."

"How about the FBI? Weren't they investigating him?" Tom was growing angrier.

"Yes for connections to terrorist groups. They had nothing that connected him to the murder of Mary Simmons, and had no motive for the murder of the Roberts girl."

"Well hell, Phil, where does that leave us now?"

"We have to go with what we have, and hope they grab this guy and keep him alive. He's killed so many people; the Feds may be able to get a confession out of him. In the meantime, we keep working to build the strongest appeal we can."

Tom hung up feeling frustrated and angry. Not only was this monster destroying his son's life, but he had also cold bloodedly murdered at least seven people along the way. It was time for him to visit John. He would want to be the one to tell him about this set back.

In spite of his son's disappointment it was a good meeting. John was a different man knowing that he was not responsible for Mary's death. He was working diligently on his appeal, documenting everything that Phil might be able to use. His enthusiasm lifted his father's spirits.

"Look what you've done so far, Dad. At least now we have hope. The knife thing was brilliant. I know you guys will get me out. It's just a matter of time."

"Well, you can bet on that, Son." Tom visited for about an hour. They talked about the case, Katherine, and the rest of the family. John blamed himself for the family problems, but he promised Tom he would make things right when he got out. Finally, John talked about Mary in a way that he had not been able to until that moment. "You would have liked her a lot, Dad. I know you would. I'm sorry she couldn't tell me about Rabbinni, but she took her work at the Law Clinic very seriously. She was a damn good attorney even before she graduated, and she would have been the best."

When they said goodbye, Tom felt a lot better than when he arrived. He was proud of his son. Life had dealt him a low blow and he was handling it like a man. Tom's resolve to get him out of this nightmare was stronger than ever.

As he drove away through the serene landscape of marshes and moss covered pines that surrounded the prison, Tom rehashed in his mind the incredible chain of events that had entangled him and his family. It was less than eight months since that first terrible phone call from John, but so much had happened in such a short time. He thought of the changes in his life. He was without a wife, without a job. His family was in shambles. His every waking moment was focused on his son's incarceration. The wonderful events that most normal families enjoyed now seemed so remote to him. His heart ached for John, who had lost his first real love under the most bizarre circumstances. And, he thought about Mary. How different things could have been if the two had married, two young attorneys, with a wonderful future ahead of them. As he drove in silence he could not seem to get Mary off his mind. It was something that John had said which was bouncing around in his brain. He mouthed John's the words. "I'm sorry she couldn't tell me about Rabbinni, but she took her Law Clinic work very seriously. She was a damn good attorney…"

CHAPTER 47

The City of New Orleans never needs much of a reason to celebrate. The annual jazz festival at the Fairgrounds Racetrack is a weeklong orgy of great music and some of the best food on earth. The French Quarter Festival in historic St. Louis Square and along the Mississippi riverfront is an annual celebration of the city's culture and history; and it's free for everyone to enjoy. The wonderful smells, sounds, and excitement of the Quarter creates a uniquely enjoyable ambiance.

The holiday season is also very special in New Orleans. The **Celebration of the Oaks** transforms City Park into an annual winter wonderland, where kids skate on artificial ice surrounded by millions of sparkling lights and displays. The city hotels compete to decorate their lobbies with elaborate Christmas themes. Even neighborhoods with strange names like **Beaugage** are transformed during Christmas with street trees filled with tiny white lights to create an atmosphere of enchantment for the thousands of visitors who drive through.

The week between Christmas Eve and New Years Eve is not a very productive time in the city except for the hospitality industry, and retail sales. Most other businesses including the city government write the week off as a time to share good cheer. The city brings in the New Year with a giant fireworks display over the Mississippi River. But, on the first day of January, while most other cities and towns are somberly reflecting on another year gone bye, New Orleans wastes no time getting its carnival season underway. That's when every man, women and child in the entire city goes insane, driven by a strange compulsion to collect more plastic beads than anyone else. On Bourbon Street beautiful women, who would never normally conduct themselves in such a way, fight the crowds to expose their breasts for yet another ten-cent string of pearls. Every week for two months oceans of people line New Orleans' streets as enormous parades with miles of floats and marching bands clog the cities arteries into massive gridlock. The spectacle is only matched by the city's remarkable ability to sweep the streets clean of tons of debris within hours after each parade passes. Indeed, anyone who has experienced it would have to agree that between Christmas and Fat Tuesday, there is nowhere else on earth like New Orleans.

It was Wednesday, December 30th and the holiday season seemed to be passing Tom Stevens by. As much as he had loved the annual gathering of family, and the wonderful warmth that seemed to fill the air during this special time, he could not feel any joy this year. There had been invitations from Chicago and Houston, and even Martha wanted him to celebrate Christmas with her in Washington, but he could not bring himself to go - not while John was away. The week passed slowly for him. Phil Townsend was out of town visiting his family, and for the first time in a long time, Tom let himself rest.

Rabbinni, however, was not resting. The festival spirit that lulled the city into a surreal euphoria provided the perfect climate for his nefarious mission. While the city was drowning in goodwill and alcoholic beverages, he had no problem carrying out his daily activities.

Acme Supply Company had won a four-year contract to supply equipment including tables and chairs to the convention center for various events. Throughout the year, Acme trucks would arrive a day before a scheduled event; and an army of workers would unload and set up the tables and chairs. The same krewe would return after the event, to clear out the building.

Acme would supply five hundred tables and five thousand chairs for the **Ball of Kings;** but this job was unlike the others. It included something extra. Every table was being specially altered for the event. Within the tables steel tube frames, workers had installed a charge of plastic explosives, sealed in airtight cylinders to defy any type of detection. Attached to each cylinder was a radio receiver. The workers belonged to Acme Supply, and Acme Supply was controlled by Abdul Rabbinni.

The charges would be timed to explode during the presidential greeting with enough force to kill every person in the convention center, but Rabbinni had other surprises planned for his own kind of celebration. From the second floor of the warehouse fifty hand held missiles would be launched to complete the total destruction of the convention center and the Mississippi River Bridge hovering above it. In the chaos that would follow Rabbinni and his faceless cohorts would simply melt into the rubble and disappear.

Tom woke the next morning still thinking about Mary Simmons. Why could he not get John's comments out of his mind? "She was a damn good attorney." He said to himself. "Of course she was a good attorney, she was tops in her class." Tom sat up slowly from the couch as he suddenly realized that no one had thought about Mary's work with Rabbinni. As any good lawyer would, she must have kept very accurate personal notes and records. Where were they? He grabbed a jacket, locked up his apartment and headed for Baton Rouge.

Life for Bob and Margaret Simmons had changed radically since the death of their daughter, Mary. They had a strong faith in God, and had come to accept their loss, but the emptiness in their lives and their hearts was difficult to overcome. The Christmas Season especially found them staring at nothing in particular as they remembered happier days in their home. The front door bell startled Margaret from one of her daydreams. "I'll get it, Dear." Her husband was in the den reading the afternoon paper. Margaret opened the door and recognized Tom immediately, but she was not able to extend her usually pleasant greeting.

"Mrs. Simmons, I'm not sure you remember me, I'm Tom Stevens." She was taken back at first. Tom Stevens might have been the last person she would expect to see at her front door.

"Yes, Mr. Stevens, I know who you are. What can we do for you?"

"Mrs. Simmons, I know my being here is a shock for you, but I must talk to you and your husband. May I come in?" There was something about Tom and Katherine Stevens that the Simmons noticed during the trial. The love and concern that they expressed for their son was not unlike the feelings that they felt for their own child. The tragedy that touched both their families had in some strange way created a spiritual bond between them.

"Yes, come in please. I'll get my husband." She showed Tom to the living room. It was neatly arranged with Victorian furniture that apparently had seen little use of late. Linen doilies were protecting the mahogany finish on the end tables and buffet. In the middle of the coffee table was an arrangement of pictures – all of Mary at various ages. Tom sat down and waited. When Bob entered the room, the two men starred at each other for a moment - Bob trying to understand what would bring this man to his home, and Tom wondering how Bob would react to his being there. Tom stood up.

"Mr. Simmons, I am so sorry to trouble you." Neither Bob nor Margaret could feel any animosity toward this man.

"That's alright, Tom why have you come?" Tom started slowly relating the events that had transpired since the trial. When he talked about

Katherine's death the Simmons both expressed genuine sympathy. As he continued, their interest grew. Tom then apologized for the sensitive nature of the subject, and then relayed the importance of the discovery that Townsend had made regarding the knife. By the time he got to Rabbinni and the subsequent killings, Margaret and Bob hung on every word. Tom had been talking for forty-five minutes, and when he finally finished all three seemed exhausted.

"You have been through a lot, Tom." Bob was now feeling closer to this man than he thought possible. "How can we help?" Tom breathed easier. These were remarkable people, and he understood the enormity of their loss.

"I need to ask you if Mary ever talked about Rabbinni, or do you know if she may have kept any records of her experience with him."

"Come with me, Tom." Bob escorted him to Mary's bedroom. As Tom expected it was meticulously clean and orderly. Margaret dusted daily and maintained the room as though Mary were still with them. "We removed everything from Mary's apartment. All of her files are here." He pointed to two three-draw oak file cabinets. "I really don't know what is in there. Neither of us has been able to look; but you are welcome to go through them. Take your time. I hope you find what you are looking for." Tom opened a top draw and was amazed to see the files in perfect order, set up alphabetically by subject matter. His fingers flipped across the top of the files and stopped at the L's where he spotted a carefully label section entitled **Law Clinic.** The largest file in the section was under **R – Rabbinni.** Tom opened the file and was stunned to see a picture of the man he had come to fear staring back at him.

Chapter 48

The files were better than Tom could have hoped for. He copied down information that he thought was critical and asked Bob if there was some way that he could secure the files for safe keeping, since they may be critical evidence in John's appeal. Bob did, in fact, have a wall safe hidden in his bedroom and agreed to do what he was asked.

Tom raced back to New Orleans. He had to talk to Phil Townsend who he hoped had returned from his family visit. Phil would know how best to use the files. Mary had taken detailed notes of every meeting with Rabbinni. She kept records of every phone call. Most importantly Mary laid out a chronology of events that she used to establish the abusive and harassing treatment that both she and Courtney were receiving at the hands of their client Mr. Rabbinni. About one of the phone calls she wrote:

Rabbinni called today at 9 P.M. Advised me that <u>he</u> was the most important concern in my life, and if I did not do whatever I had to do to win his case, he would see that there would be no other cases for me.

There were other records that strongly supported the possibility that Abdul Rabbinni killed Mary Simmons. Surely there would be enough information to cast reasonable doubt on John's guilt.

When he arrived home, the New Orleans's Police were waiting for him. They had found a calendar in Professor Norton's office showing that Tom had met with the professor on the day he was killed. They wanted to know why.

Under normal circumstances, Tom did not have much use for the New Orleans Police Department. In recent years it had earned the reputation as being one of the most corrupt in the country. Recent headlines reported the scandalous activities of an officer Len Davis and his brothers in blue, who terrorized the city at will, while operating a lucrative drug operation. Davis was finally busted for murder by an FBI sting operation. Since then a new police chief was making some progress in cleaning up the department, but the general consensus was that he had along way to go.

Tom had a dilemma. If he told them why he visited Norton, he would have to get into what he knew about detective Crawford and Rabbinni, and he might be forced to reveal what he found in Baton Rouge. He feared what might happen to that information in the wrong hands. Who knew what contacts a man like Rabbinni might have - especially in this police department. He did not want to jeopardize John's case in any way, but more importantly, with Rabbinni still out there, he did not want to put any more lives in danger- including his own

"I met Norman when my son was at Tulane. We both loved to fish. We used to swap fish stories all the time. I've been thinking about taking some night courses at Tulane and I stopped by to see Norm, while I was on campus. Just a social call. It's a terrible thing what happened to him. He was a good guy."

"Do you have any idea who might have wanted him dead?" One of the detectives seemed remotely interested in what Tom's answer might be.

"No, can't say that I do. I didn't really know anything about his personal life. Just fishing. That's all." That was a good enough answer for the cops who told Tom to be sure to contact them if he had any more information.

"I sure will. Thanks for stopping by."

Tom watched them drive off before calling Phil Townsend. There was no answer. He left a message to call as soon as possible. Tom was pacing. Nervous energy would not let him sit down. He went to the kitchen and made a pot of coffee. At the kitchen table he sipped the coffee and read through the notes that he made in Baton Rouge. He noted the content of several calls that Mary had returned to Rabbinni. He wished he had Phil's instincts. Phil would see things in Mary's files that escaped Tom. He would be able to connect the dots, that only frustrated Tom.

To keep himself occupied, Tom listed all incoming and outgoing phone calls in chronological order. He noted the dates and the time each was made and received. He briefly noted the content of each call as Mary reported it. Rabbinni said this. Rabbinni said that. Mary said this. Mary said that. Would this help Phil somehow? He wondered.

When he finished, he stared at the sheet of paper in front of him, and sipped his coffee. Then suddenly, like the first time one of those three-dimensional puzzles in the Sunday paper comes into focus, a broad smile covered Tom's face. He was starring at phone numbers that Mary used to reach Abdul Rabbinni. Those numbers must be attached to addresses and possibly still to Rabbinni, himself. He started dialing the phone. Two numbers were disconnected. One rang with no answer. The fourth was answered by a very pleasant recorded voice.

You have reached Acme Supply Company. Our office is opened from 7 A.M. to 5 P.M. Monday through Friday with warehouse service until noon on Saturdays.

Tom scribbled the name on a pad and grabbed for the phone book. He read out loud. "Acme Supply Company, 1830 Tchopitoulas Street." The warehouse was at 330 Magazine Street. He was somewhat familiar with the areas. The Magazine Street address was in the old warehouse district that was undergoing a renaissance of sorts as developers were discovering the potential value of converting the old buildings to upscale residential uses. But, many of the buildings were abandoned while others were being converted to nightclubs. Some like the Acme building still operated as a warehouse. The Tchopitoulas Street address was in a desolate area behind the St Thomas Housing Project - the site of many murders and other criminal activity through the years. It was not an area where you would want to run out of gas - especially at night.

It was going on ten o'clock. Darkness covered the city, as the nightlife came alive. Tom tried Townsend's number again. Still nothing. His better judgment told him to sit tight, and go over his findings with Phil when he returned. But, another side of Tom had grown impatient. What would it hurt to at least find the Acme addresses? He'd take a drive by and be back by eleven.

CHAPTER 49

Before leaving, Tom scratched out a note to Phil Townsend and gathered up his papers into a manila envelope. He decided to stop by Phil's apartment before looking for Acme Supply. When Phil was still not home, Tom pushed his envelope through the mail slot, so that Phil would have his notes as soon as he returned. He then set out to find Acme Supply.

He drove up Canal Street toward the River Walk shopping area and the Hilton Hotel. Before turning right on Magazine Street, he passed by the land casino which had promised to bring millions to the city, but now sat abandoned like a grounded rusting tanker. Its construction was abruptly halted when the developer's could not pay their bills. No one was surprised. Permits for the project were tied to ridiculous income projections, which the city and state would share. True to classic Louisiana politics, there had been millions in pay offs to guarantee the votes to support the project. The real plan, of course, was to get the project started, and then, under the threat of bankruptcy, renegotiate a new, more favorable deal, that would put more money in the developers' pockets and cover all of the pay offs. The big losers, when the doors opened would be the taxpayers, who ultimately would benefit little from the casino.

Tom passed under the Mississippi River Bridge from Magazine to Tchopitoulas Street. The riverfront was on his left hidden behind a flood barrier. On his right was an assortment of dilapidated light industrial and office buildings. He drove slowly trying to read addresses that were not there. Then suddenly on a corner under a streetlight he saw: **Acme Supply Company.** The building was small, about fifteen hundred square feet on one floor. Off the rear corner of the building a barbed wire chain link fence ran around the perimeter of a parking area. The area confined a fleet of Acme trucks. The building blended well with the depressed neighborhood. Its stucco siding needed paint; and its wood trim was being consumed by Formosan termites. Tom saw nothing unusual about the building except the video cameras mounted high on each corner. No one seemed to use guard dogs any more since the Times Picayune carried a story about a break-in at a construction site where the crooks took what they wanted, and then stole the two vicious Pit Bull watch dogs, as well. He drove around the block and headed toward Magazine Street.

The warehouse was in the shadows of the Morial Convention Center. It was two stories high and it covered most of a city block. As Tom drove around the block he noticed that all entrances except those on Magazine Street were boarded up. In another life the building must have housed some thriving industry, but clearly, whatever went on inside now did not utilize the entire building, and all service entrances were restricted to the front.

As Tom was about to return to his apartment, he noticed an area on the second floor where the lights were still burning. He looked up and saw a silhouette pass behind a shade. His watch told him it was ten minutes to eleven. "Someone's working late." he said to himself. For some reason he did not understand, he parked his car about a hundred feet up the road and walked back to the building. While passing by the front door, he tried the doorknob. Not surprisingly it was locked. There was a series of overhead doors along Magazine Street. Tom lifted himself onto the loading dock and casually tried one of the overheads. Locked also. Now, trying to appear like he might have some reason for being in the area, Tom continued down Magazine to the end of the building, and turned the corner. Old cracked and clouded double hung windows lined the street. As he walked straight ahead past the boarded doorways and shattered windows his eyes looked for an opening. At the next corner, the streetlight was broken leaving the rear of the building in total darkness. Turning into the darkness Tom approached a window and stepped up onto the sill. With a quick shot of his elbow, he smashed a light of glass and reached in to release the lock. The window had not been opened in years but he was able to lift it high enough to roll his two hundred and thirty pound body into the building. "I'm way too old for this shit." He said, as he lowered the window and checked to see if anyone had seen him. A drunk in the doorway across the street seemed mildly interested.

The inside was full of cobwebs, and from the moonlight penetrating the dirty windows, Tom could see ghostly footprints of heavy machines that were once mounted to the oil soaked wooden floor. He made his way through the building toward the front trying not to make the floorboards squeak. A sliding, metal clad fire door separated the vacant back end of the building from the front. As Tom slowly rolled the door opened, he could see crates of machinery and equipment stacked to the ceiling. Next to a cage-like freight elevator that he had no interest in using, was a wooden stairway. The treads were worn from years of foot traffic. Slowly and quietly, he climbed the stairs to the second floor.

He could hear the voices coming from behind a closed door. They were arguing in a Middle Eastern dialect. Tom carefully approached the door to see if he could understand anything from the conversation. A tattered shade was drawn down on the inside of the office door. He peaked through a tear that allowed him to see three men from the neck up. He recognized the one in the middle from his photograph. It was Rabbinni.

Adrenalin started pumping through his body. His only thought was to get the hell out of the building and tell someone that he had found Rabbinni. But, before he could turn around the butt end of an assault rifle came crashing down on his skull. Bright lights sparkled momentarily behind his eyelids before the blackness came. Tom slumped to the floor.

CHAPTER 50

Phil Townsend returned home at 10 o'clock Wednesday morning. He picked up a load of mail that had piled up in his front hall and flipped through it. Separating personal letters and familiar professional envelopes from the bundle, he tossed the rest on the dining room table. He'd been away since December 24th, and, although he had enjoyed a reunion with his folks and relatives, he was glad to be back in the solitude of his oversized apartment on Esplanade Ave.

The old Victorian house had once been a private home, but through the years its graceful floor plan had been chopped up into four apartments. Still, each unit had two big bedrooms, a good size kitchen, and one and a half baths. Phil especially liked the formal dining room, with a big table that he had converted into his home office. Esplanade Avenue was a comfortable street bordering the lower end of the French Quarter. The street and the apartment provided Phil with refuge from his hectic life, as a public defender.

As he opened the mail, he punched his answering machine. He heard what he expected to hear. Call after call from clients and fellow attorneys. His mother had called before Christmas asking him where he was. Toward the end of the tape, there was a call from Tom Stevens. Tom seemed anxious to talk with him, so Phil immediately returned the call. There was no answer. He'd try again later.

It was New Year's Eve. One of the reasons Townsend had returned was to attend a party at the Bella Luna, to be hosted by one of the largest law firms in the city. It was an annual event and as always it promised to be a grand affair. He was looking forward to having some fun before emerging himself back into his impossible workload, which was the other reason he had returned. His job was tough, and didn't pay much compared to what the corporate pinstripe suits were earning, but he got great satisfaction from it.

He opened a few more letters, before changing his clothes and leaving for his office at the courthouse, which he knew would be closed for the afternoon. With no phone calls and interruptions he would have a perfect opportunity to get a jump on the backlog of work that no doubt had piled up on his desk. As he locked the front door, Tom Steven's envelope remained unopened on the dining room table.

*   *   *   *

Tom woke to the morning sun shining through the warehouse windows. He had a pounding headache. The blow to his head left a good size contusion. Heavy rope bound him to a wooden chair.

"Welcome, Mr. Stevens. I am so happy that you have come to our little party. We were not expecting you." Rabbinni was addressing him like an old friend. Tom saw the contents of his wallet strewn across the floor. "To what do we owe this pleasure?" Tom squinted and decided to try a *Mickey the Mope* routine.

"I saw the light on last night, and thought I'd ask about some storage space."

"Ah, yes, some storage space. And you broke into my building to inquire about some storage space?" Rabbinni was circling Tom with hands clasped behind his back.

"Well, the door was locked."

"Yes Mr. Stevens. You see, we lock the door to keep people out, but now that you are in, perhaps you would be so kind to tell us who you are, and why you are here."

"I'm nobody. I was just looking for some storage space." Rabbinni suddenly whipped the back of his hand across Tom's face.

"Do you think I am a fool? You will tell us who you are, Mr. Stevens. I promise you that. Take him." Two men grabbed Tom under his arms and lifted him off the chair. His hands were tied behind his back, and his feet were tied at the ankles. Rabbinni lowered a chain fall from a ceiling beam, while one of his men shoved a piece of pipe behind Tom's back and under his arms. With the chain fall hook fastened around the pipe, Rabbinni pushed a button that slowly lifted Tom off the floor and left him hanging ten feet above his captors.

"Perhaps, if you hang around for a while, Mr. Stevens you will feel like telling us who you are." Rabbinni laughed at his pun, as Tom felt the hook bore into his back. He was definitely too old for this shit.

*   *   *   *

Townsend worked until five thirty, and then returned home to shower and prepare for his party. He had tried calling Tom Stevens twice from his office with no success. He thought maybe he had returned to Bay St. Louis for New Years Eve.

The Bella Luna was located next to the French Market. The food was very good, but the restaurant was more famous for hosting private parties.

Townsend turned his Honda over to a complimentary valet on Decatur Street, and took the elevator to the second floor restaurant. He was alone. The restaurant was long and narrow with an entire wall of bay windows overlooking the Mississippi River. Serving stations were set up at both ends of the room, with a jazz combo in the middle. Festively decorated, Linen covered tables, set for eight, were randomly set up on the floor leaving plenty of room to dance and mill about. Opposite the window wall were several sets of French doors opening onto a balcony that looked down on Decatur Street. The street was beginning to swell with rowdy New Year's Eve amateurs.

Townsend found his place setting and made his way to the nearest serving station. Starting with Shrimp Romalade, and a cup of sea food gumbo, he moved along filling his plate with herb pasta cooked in garlic and oil, rosemary roasted lamb chops, blackened Cajun sword fish, prime rib, fried catfish, julienne vegetables, fresh fruit, mixed cheeses and fresh French bread. On his way back to his table, he snagged a glass of Black Opal Chardonnay from the tray of a tuxedoed waiter.

The long mahogany bar by the entrance remained open all evening, serving beer, wine and mixed drinks. Some of the city's most high-powered lawyers stationed themselves at the bar sipping 15-year-old single malt scotch and smoking hand rolled cigars. Phil finished his plate and returned for a few more, cooked to perfection, lamb chops. He also helped himself to a piece of praline cheesecake, a rare treat that he seldom allowed himself.

By eleven o'clock the party was in full swing. Although the food stations remained opened to serve the late arrivals, most guests had eaten their fill and were trying to dance it off on the crowded dance floor. The band was playing: *Do you know what it means to miss New Orleans?*, while several over-served Harry Connick want-a-bes sang along.

Phil stepped out on the balcony for some fresh air. He dated off and on, when he had time, but he was not ready for any long-term commitments. Flying solo just seemed to make his life a lot less complicated. Besides, there had been someone special in his life once, but he made a bad decision and she ended up marrying someone else.

"Phil it's nice to see you." She stepped up behind him, and took him by surprise. Phil turned. Anne Murray, not the singer, was a colleague that Phil often opposed in the courtroom. The two had great respect for each other.

"Anne, I didn't know you were coming. You look beautiful." And she did. Phil was used to seeing her in business suits and tied back hair. Tonight she was wearing a low cut silk teal dress, hemmed about four inches above the knee with a very sexy slit up the side. Her long auburn hair blew freely in the night breeze. Anne had lost her husband in a plane crash three years earlier, and like Phil, her work seemed to be the most important thing in her life at the time.

"Thank you. I don't usually come to these things, but I heard this was something special, and it is. I'm glad I came." She leaned her shapely body against the balcony wall and took a sip of wine.

"Oh, this is always great. I wouldn't miss it. I'm glad you came too." The two shared another glass of wine, and allowed themselves to flow with the ambience of the evening. They were very comfortable in each other's company. At twelve o'clock they were on the dance floor, and for some reason at the stroke of midnight a long and tender kiss seemed for both of them the right thing to do.

Phil woke up the next morning in his own bed, alone. It had been a wonderful evening that awakened feelings that both he and Anne had not felt in along time. But at the end of the night both agreed it would be a good idea to move slowly toward a relationship.

CHAPTER 51

Eight blindfolded men and women were being lead into the middle of a large outdoor amphitheater that looked like a bullring. The curious procession lead to a large round table where each person took a seat. The blindfolds were removed, and the guests marveled at the magnificent meal that had been prepared for them. They drank wine and ate heartily. And then suddenly, without any warning the table exploded, ripping the people into shreds of blood and guts and bone. Tom, stunned and unable to believe what he was watching, turned his head away from the TV monitor, as scraps of metal, and human debris showered down on the infield. Rabbinni smiled.

Rabbinni did not leave Tom hanging from the rafters all night. After several hours he lowered him so that Tom could watch the videotape that was prepared to demonstrate the destructive potential of his insidious exploding tables. The unsuspecting guests were former Rabbinni followers who had become disloyal to his cause. Tom had no idea what he was viewing, but his appreciation for the viciousness of his captor was taking on new dimensions.

"Are you ready now to tell us who you are Mr. Stevens?"

"Look, I told you. I'm nobody. I'm a salesman. That's all. I should not have broken into your building. I'm sorry about that."

"Oh yes. Indeed you are. And you will be more so." Rabbinni nodded to the two goons who took turns beating Tom unconscious. They dragged him into a six by ten closet formerly used to keep paint and flammable materials separated from other manufacturing materials. Leaving him there in a pile, on the floor, they locked the door.

CHAPTER 52

It was noontime, the day before the **Ball of Kings.** The city was overflowing with out-of-town party lovers, and visiting dignitaries. There was not an empty hotel room to be found anywhere in the city. Barricades lined the New Orleans Streets. The barricades would be a part of the cityscape until the end of Carnival Season.

The New Orleans Police were not the best crime fighters, but they did know how to control crowds. As with so many major events that took place in the Crescent City including a World's Fair, numerous Super Bowls, political conventions and, of course, its unique Mardi Gras, the police would have streets guerdoned off to restrict and direct traffic in and around the city. Access to the Convention Center was being strictly controlled. Security guards were placed at every entrance, checking the identification of service people and technicians who were preparing the facility for the big event. No one was allowed to enter without prior approval and proper identification. Rabbinni's people moved freely in and out of the massive building all day long without incident.

Across town, Phil showered, made some coffee, and retrieved the morning paper. Along with the paper he brought the bundle of unopened mail to the kitchen table. He again sorted the envelopes tossing several pieces, unopened, into the trashcan. The manila envelope was making its way to the top of the pile, when the phone rang.

"I understand that the Riverview Restaurant at the top of the Marriott has a great jazz brunch. Want to join me?" it was Anne. He'd been thinking about her all morning.

"Anne, That's a great idea. I know the manager. Let me call for a table."

"Great. Why don't we meet in the lobby at 1 o'clock?"

"I'll be there. I'm so glad you called." Phil looked at his watch, and dialed Tom Stevens again. He hung up after the fourth ring, and dialed another number. "In Bay St. Louis, please, a listing for Thomas Stevens?" The phone rang twice. "Come on, Tom. Where the hell are you?" He hung up, shaved, put on a navy blue turtleneck with a camel hair sport jacket and black slacks, and headed for the Marriott.

$$* \qquad * \qquad * \qquad *$$

John Stevens had been trying to reach his father for two days. He expected a call from him on New Years Eve, and he was now finding it very strange that his dad had not called all day long. It was getting close to five o'clock. He decided to call Phil Townsend.

Phil and Anne, after a wonderful brunch, decided to spend the rest of the day together. They had driven out to the art museum in City Park to see a Faberge exhibit. Anne was fascinated with the diamond and gold incrusted ornamental eggs. Phil had a hard time understanding how such wealth could be squandered on useless nick-knacks. After the exhibit they drove out to Joe's Crab Shack on Lake Pontchartrain to have a drink and watch the sun go down. John's call reached Phil there.

"Hello, Mr. Townsend, this is John Stevens."

"John, How are you doing?"

"I'm okay, but, I was wondering about my dad. Have you talked with him lately?"

"Funny you should ask, John. I have been trying to reach him myself. He left me a message. Said it was urgent. You haven't heard from him either?"

"No I haven't, and I think it is strange that he hasn't called. I'm a little concerned."

"I don't blame you. Tell you what. Let me track him down and see that he gives you a call." Phil was beginning to share John's concern. John hung up more worried, now that his father had something urgent to tell Phil. Anne noticed that the call had made Phil uneasy.

"Trouble?"

"No. I don't think so. Actually, I don't know. I seem to have lost a client." Phil gave Anne some background on the case. "I think I better take a ride by his apartment. I'm sorry Anne."

"Hey, Phil, don't worry about it. I understand. Why don't I go with you?"

"Okay, let's go. It shouldn't take long." Without waiting for a check, he left a ten-dollar bill on the table for the two drinks

The front door of Tom's apartment was locked. Townsend peered through the window on the front porch, but could see no one. He examined the window. The lock was a lever that clamped the upper and lower sash together. With a credit card slipped between the sashes, and a little pressure, he was able to disengage the lock.

"Excuse me, counselor." Anne tapped him on the shoulder. "Isn't this called breaking and entering?"

"It is indeed, and you are my accomplice." He lifted the window and climbed throw. Anne waited on the porch for him to open the door.

Phil checked the apartment for anything that looked suspicious. There was nothing. Certainly no sign of a struggle. Tom's bed was made. Nothing seemed out of place.

"Does this mean anything, Phil?" Anne was looking at some papers on the kitchen table. Phil took a look. Tom had written an address in Baton Rouge, with the name Robert Simmons. Phil knew the name well. He called information for a number. Bob Simmons answered the phone. After introducing himself and explaining why he was calling, he asked about Tom.

"Yes, he was here. He went through my daughter's files and made some notes. He seemed pleased with what he found."

"Did he take the files?" Phil was getting anxious.

"No, He asked me to keep them in my safe."

"Do you mind if I come and look at them."

"No but can it wait until tomorrow, its getting a little late for my wife and I." Phil wanted to leave for Baton Rouge immediately, but he certainly did not want to upset Bob Simmons.

"Tomorrow will be fine. Early. Thank you Mr. Simmons."

CHAPTER 53

At seven o'clock on the morning of the **Ball of Kings**, a small fleet of Acme Supply trucks rolled up to the loading docks at the rear of the convention center. A clean-cut driver approached the Security Chief with a clipboard. The two signed some papers, and several security officers stood by as the table and chairs were off loaded and stacked inside the convention center.

Tom was in pain as he awoke on the paint stained floor. The room was dark with the exception of a patch of light that penetrated an opening around the doorjamb. He lifted himself to his feet and squinted through the crack. Rabbinni's men were positioning steel drums in front of the windows along Magazine Street. The drums were labeled: **Solvent**, with a warning advising caution due to flammability. By three in the afternoon, more than a hundred barrels would be in place; and, indeed, they would be filled with thousands of gallons of oily heavy scented paint remover.

Some time in the afternoon, there would be a routine security sweep of the buildings around the convention center. Dogs would be set free to seek out explosives of any kind, and there was a good chance that the dogs would find the barrels. Rabbinni had anticipated that, and directed his workers to open any barrel upon request. The odds were twenty to one against opening any of the five barrels that contained the missiles. Even if those particular barrels were opened, metal inserts that held six inches of solvent at the top would make them appear no different than the rest. The inserts could be easily removed to expose the dry cavity, containing ten rockets and launches in each of the five barrels. The anticipated security check and clearance of the building was just one more step in Rabbinni's well thought out plan.

Phil Townsend was knocking on the Simmons' door in Baton Rouge at nine o'clock in the morning. Bob and Margaret, as usual, were gracious. Margaret had a pot of coffee brewing and some corn muffins coming out of the oven. Phil accepted a hot cup, and a muffin, while he exchanged pleasantries with his hosts.

"I suppose you will want to get to Mary's records?" Bob could sense that Townsend was anxious to get on with the purpose of his visit.

"If you don't mind?" He smiled and let Bob show him to the wall safe. As he turned the pages of the files, he was amazed at what Tom had found. Document after document built a case against Rabbinni. Mary's records were impeccable. "Bob, did Tom remove anything?"

"No, he only made notes."

"And did you remove the files from your daughters apartment yourself?"

"Yes, Margaret and I did. Why do you ask?"

"These files will be called into evidence in John Stevens appeal. It is very important that we are able to show that they have not been tampered with or altered in any way. I would like to ask your permission to copy them in your presence. Then I will ask you to secure them again. Can we do that?"

"Yes of course. I understand how important they could be. I have a copy machine at the office. Why don't we go there?" You won't be disturbed.

By noon, Phil was on his way back to New Orleans with a complete copy of the Rabbinni file. He had seen enough to know how much it would help John, but he was wondering now what might be in the file that would help him find Tom. He called Anne and asked her to meet him at his apartment. When he arrived, she was waiting for him on the front step with a whole muffuletta from the Central Deli on Decatur Street. The massive sandwich with its fresh Italian cold cuts and special olive garnish was another unique New Orleans delicacy, and certainly large enough for both their lunches. While Anne prepared the muffuletta in the kitchen, Tom laid out the contents of the file on the dining room table. He made piles of legal proceedings, minutes of meetings, status reports, correspondence, phone calls, and memoranda. At the top of the piles he placed a photocopy of Rabbinni's picture.

Anne served the sandwiches with two bottles of cold beer, as Phil eyes went from one pile to another.

"There's a lot of good stuff here, Anne, but Tom saw something that he said was urgent - something that may have gotten him into trouble. I'm going to start with these meeting minutes. I'd like you to read through the correspondence." As they washed the muffelleta down with the beer, they began to get a first hand report of the encounter that Mary Simmons had with Abdul Rabbinni. She may very well be responsible for bringing this monster to justice from her grave, Phil thought.

The ceremonies at the convention center were to get underway at seven in the evening with the grand procession of the Kings and their lavish courts. Each would be introduced and escorted to his throne at the head table. With the kings seated, the guests of honor would be introduced and seated. The King of Rex one of the oldest and most prestigious krewes would serve at as Master of Ceremonies. There would be greetings and formal decrees exchanged, before a banquet fit for kings would be served to the thousands of loyal subjects who were lucky enough to acquire a five hundred dollar admission ticket. In the grand tradition of Mardi Gras those in attendance would spare no expense in displaying themselves in the most outrageous costumes, and formal regalia. After dinner, the President of the United States, Bill Clinton, would bring his greetings. As planned by the organizers, the affair would go well into the next morning with dancing and top name entertainment. But on Magazine Street, there were other plans under-way that would bring the festivities to an abrupt halt during the President's address.

With the radio-controlled detonation of the explosives inside each table, Rabbinni's men would launch a fifty-missile strike on the build-ing and surrounding infrastructure. A prime target would be the mas-sive concrete supports for the Mississippi River Bridge, which were incorporated into the design of the convention center. Rabbinni savored visions of the bridge's superstructure crashing down on the rubble of the convention center in a final act of total devastation.

By five o'clock, Phil and Anne had been over every piece of paper in the file. They had not seen what Tom saw, nor were they able to reach him after repeated calls to all of Tom's phone numbers. Phil sat starring at the material before him, his mind working to make some connection. Exasperated, he stood up and walked to the kitchen to stretch his legs. Anne had moved the unopened pile of mail from the table to the kitchen counter, where it now caught Phil's eye. He picked it up to dis-card the remaining junk mail. The manila envelope had not interested him earlier. With no address, he assumed it was another hand delivered solicitation for some amazing new product, or time-share resort. "What are we missing Anne?" He said while fingering the envelope.

"I don't know. Maybe he just got excited about the file in general. Maybe there wasn't any particular thing."

"Maybe you are right." Phil opened the manila envelope and examined the contents. "Oh my God."

CHAPTER 54

At three that afternoon a crew of workers from Acme Supply returned to the convention center to set up the tables and chairs. Each worker had the proper identification. By five o' clock, the job was complete, and the building contained enough explosive charges to blow the roof into the Mississippi River.

As anticipated, a secret service security detail arrived at the warehouse at three in the afternoon. It was officially closed due to the restricted traffic in the area, but an elderly watchman, carefully chosen by Rabbinni, let them in. They swept through the building with two German Shepherds. The dogs found nothing on the first floor. On the second floor, when the dogs reacted to the odor of the solvent, an agent asked the watchman about the contents of the barrels. The watchman said he knew nothing more than what was stenciled on the sides. As the agent pulled against the top of a randomly selected barrel, he immediately felt the weight of fifty-five gallons of liquid. He then walked along the front row of barrels tapping each one with a cigarette lighter. Rabbinni had not expected this simple method of detecting any differences in the contents. The watchman tried not to show his nervousness as the agent approached a barrel that would surely produce a distinctively different sound. Suddenly the agents hand held radio squelched, interrupting his tapping. The security team on the first floor reported that nothing unusual was found. The agent stopped what he was doing, and responded. "Roger, clear on the second floor also." He then abruptly left the barrels and regrouped with the others who were proceeding to the next building. The entire sweep took only twenty minutes. During that time none of the agents opened the door to Tom's closet, where they would have found him bound and gagged just for the occasion.

*   *   *   *

"What's the matter, Phil?" Anne was startled by Phil's response to the contents of Tom's envelope.

"I feel like such a jerk." This is from Tom. He has summarized Mary's files, and gone looking for Rabbinni. I've had this for two days, damn it. Tom must have found something. He could be in trouble. Maybe that's why we haven't been able to reach him."

"What are you going to do?"

"I have got to get this information to the FBI. Will you help me, Anne?"

"Yes, of course. What can I do?"

"I want you to take this to Camp Street." He wrote the address on the envelope, along with the name of an FBI agent whom Phil had had some dealings with. "Ted Nolan will know what to do with this information. I am going to look for Tom. I'll stay in touch with you by cell. This is extremely important, Anne. This city is filled with foreign dignitaries, and Clinton himself is scheduled to be at the Convention Center. I hate to think that Rabbinni is out there somewhere."

*   *   *   *

Tom managed to remove the rag from his mouth by hooking it around a nail protruding from the wall. He then used the nail to loosen the knot that bound his hands behind his back. Outside the doors he could hear Rabbinni and his men moving about quickly. He struggled for half an hour before the rope began to loosen. With his wrists free, he quickly untied his ankles. Footsteps were approaching the door. He quickly wrapped the ropes around his legs and fell back into the corner with his hands behind his back. Rabbinni's man looked in to find Tom just as he had left him.

"Soon, my friend. It will be over for you." Tom feigned semi-consciousness, as the guard closed and relocked the steel door. Tom listened as he walked away. Back on his feet, he again peered through the crack in the doorjamb. He could see at least ten men unpacking the rocket launches from the barrels. A firing station was being set up at each of the ten windows across the front of the building. From the second floor, there was a clear shot at the convention center. It was approaching six-fifteen. Tom could also see Rabbinni and a cohort standing in front of a control panel. He did not know that the panel was tuned to the radio receivers that would detonate the explosives inside the Convention Center. "This can't be a good thing." Tom said to himself.

*   *   *   *

Phil Townsend found Acme Supply Co. on Tchoupitoulas Street. There was a fleet of trucks in the yard, but the office did not appear to be open. He pulled along side the building and got out of his car. The front door was locked. As he walked back to his car he noticed that the chain lock on the yard was hanging loose. Phil stooped down and squeezed his athletic frame between the fence post and the gate. An old wooden door leading from the yard to the office had seen better days. Phil was able to kick a panel out and reach inside to throw a deadbolt open. Once inside the building he quickly moved from room to room. He could sense that Tom was not there, but he was attracted to a city map on the wall. Someone had circle an area around the convention center, and Phil was reminded that the warehouse was located in that vicinity.

*   *   *   *

Tom tried to loosen the boards that enclosed him. It was an old building, constructed with old dimensioned lumber, and the walls were built with solid two-inch planks. He could not budge them. As he looked around his small prison, he saw a five-gallon container in the corner, left over from some long ago painting project. He lifted the can and found that it was almost full, and weighed about twenty pounds. His mind started working fast now. Tying together the two pieces of rope that bound his hands and feet, he fastened one end around the handle of the paint can and threw the other over a beam in the ceiling. He then hoisted the can up to the beam six feet above the door. The nail in the wall that helped him loosen the ropes also served now to tie off the other end. With the trap set, he positioned himself where he could see through the crack and waited for captors to open the door.

At six o'clock, limousines started arriving at the Convention Center. Parking lots for miles around were beginning to fill. The streets in and out of the downtown area were bumper to bumper as the police redirected frustrated drivers away from their intended destinations. Phil Townsend sat in a traffic jam at Lee Circle. Horns were blowing all around him as irate drivers tried to relieve their anger. Phil abandoned his car and set out on foot toward the spotlights illuminating the night sky from the top of the convention center.

Rabbinni's men were working methodically to set up the rocket launching stations within the warehouse. Rabbinni himself was setting timing devises on a control panel that would detonate the explosions inside the convention center. At the top of the control panel, a stop clock was clicking off the minutes to eight o'clock. Tom could take in the whole operation from his crack in the doorjamb. He had seen the destruction that a single exploding table could cause and suddenly he became aware of the annihilation that was being played out before his eyes.

CHAPTER 55

Inside the convention center, lavish decorations accented the elevated head table. The convention floor was sectioned off into areas designated for each of the various crews that were represented by their kings at the head table. Costumed and formally dressed guests rambled around the enormous interior looking for their designated tables. As the cavernous ballrooms began to fill, an orchestra played traditional New Orleans Jazz from a center stage.

According to schedule, all attendees should be in their seats by seven. A royal procession would lead the Kings to their thrones by seven-thirty. President Clinton would be introduced at eight-o'clock, when New Orleans' legendary Fats Domino would present him with a gold plated saxophone. Unknown to the celebrities and thousands of invited guests, the convention center, at a touch of Rabbinni's finger, would then be blown to smithereens at one minute past eight, and a rocket attack on the surrounding area would reign destruction and chaos on the city.

Phil Townsend was running through the streets, toward Magazine. He too had figured out that if Rabbinni were in town, the convention center would be his target. Ahead of him, about a hundred yards on the right he could see **Acme Supply Co.** stenciled in ten foot letters on the side of a red brick building.

At quarter to eight, Rabbinni clicked on a TV monitor that his inside people had tied into the security cameras within the Convention Center. He was able to view the entire floor as the crowd applauded the arrival of the spectacular parade of kings. He watched intently as the crowd settled down anticipating the introduction of the President. There was another eruption as the one and only Fats Domino arrived sitting at a gold piano on top of an enormous float.

At Rabbinni's command, ten men shouldered the rocket launches and took position behind the windows along Magazine Street. As Rabbinni watched the clock begin its last five-minute countdown, he signaled his men to remove Tom from the storage room. He wanted the added pleasure of watching Tom's reaction to the destruction before killing him. From within the closet, Tom's heart was pounding as the men approached the door. He crouched down next to the nail in the wall, without the slightest idea what he would do when his trap was sprung.

At the same time, Phil Townsend and a squad of FBI agents were breaking down the first floor door to the warehouse. Anne had delivered the package, and as Phil expected, Ted Nolan instantly recognized the imminent danger.

The door to the storage room burst open. Tom let loose the rope, and the five gallon paint can fell directly onto the head of the lead man, knocking him unconscious. Before the second man could react Tom broke from a squatting position like he had not done since his college football days. He drove his head into the chest of the second man, knocking him to the floor. Tom continued his charge straight at Rabbinni who was stumbling to get out of the way of the oncoming freight train. He could not. Tom plowed into Rabbinni, smashing him and the control panel into the brick wall.

"Fire, Fire." Lying on his back, Rabbinni ordered his men to commence the rocket attack. Two rockets were released, hitting their designated target, the Mississippi River Bridge. The super structure buckled, as concrete began to fall from the spans. Suddenly a spray of automatic fire from Federal agents shattered the wall of windows striking two of Rabbinni's men and causing the others to drop down behind the barrels of solvent, interrupting the rocket launching.

Tom rolled over, dazed from smashing into the wall, and saw Rabbinni next to him, struggling to regain his footing. Rolling onto his back, he planted the heel of his shoe directly on Rabbinni's jaw, sending him reeling back against the brick wall. The FBI agents and the rest of Rabbinni's men were now engaged in a fierce firefight as bullets ricocheted throughout the building. Tom saw the control panel on the floor, and low-crawled over to it. He had no idea how it worked but he knew he had to get it out of harms way. With bullets flying overhead, he held the panel to his chest and crouched down at the end of the row of barrels, he was on the fifty-yard line watching the exchange of fire.

Twenty feet away from him, one of Rabbinni's men took a round right between his eyes, and fell immediately to the floor, leaving a rocket launcher unprotected at his feet. Tom set the control panel down and scrambled to the launcher. Grabbing the launcher he duck-walked back to the protection of the steel barrels. Two of Nolan's men were down, and with inferior firepower, Nolan signaled for his men to drop back to the stairwell. Tom broke for the storage room, carrying the control panel in one hand and the rocket in the other. He could see Nolan's men were retreating down the stairway. When they were out of sight Tom hoisted the launcher to his shoulder and took aim. The rocket landed in the middle of the solvent barrels setting off tremendous blast and fireball that blew out the remaining windows and scorched everything within 200 feet. No one remaining on the second floor survived the blast.

No one but Tom. He had positioned himself in the storage room behind the steel door leaving a six-inch opening. When he fired the rocket, he pulled the steel door closed, protecting himself and the control panel from the blast. One by one the remaining rockets exploded. With the building burning furiously now, he tucked the panel under his arm and ran for the stairway. The smoke was heavy and the heat was unbearable.

On the ground level, Ted Nolan, Phil Townsend, and Anne Murray watched in horror, from across Magazine Street, as the flames engulfed the second story of the warehouse. Phil put his arm around Anne and began to move back from the heat when suddenly he saw an overhead door open on the loading dock. Tom Stevens walked out onto the loading platform holding the black panel. He took a deep breath of fresh air, and collapsed.

CHAPTER 56

Three weeks later Tom and John Stevens along with Phil Townsend and Bradford Stern stood before Judge Quinton. Townshends request for an appeal had been quickly granted and remanded back to the trial judge. Following the fire, the FBI took possession of Rabbinni's control panel and quickly disarmed its terrible destructive potential. Tom Stevens was already being cited for his extraordinary act of courage in saving thousands of lives including the President's.

Townsend had prepared a brilliant summary of the case, establishing the probability of Rabbinni's being responsible for the deaths of Courtney Roberts, Allison McKay, Sergeant Crawford, Professor Norton and Mary Simmons. He also demonstrated that because of the position of his palm print on the murder weapon, John Steven's could not have inflicted the fatal stab wound to Mary Simmons. Both Bradford Stern and Judge Quinton had read the appeal transcript.

"Mr. Townsend," Judge Quinton addressed the Defense Consul. "you have made a motion in light of new evidence in this case and circumstances occurring over the past several weeks that all charges against your client, Mr. John Stevens, relating to the murder of Mrs. Mary Simmons be dropped."

"We do respectfully request that, Your Honor."

"Mr. Stern, what is the State's response to this motion?" Stern paused to looked at John Stevens and at his father standing behind him.

"Your Honor, in light of the circumstances, the State of Louisiana is pleased to drop all charges in the matter." John turned to his father, and the two men hugged like they had not done since John was a boy. The two men then grabbed hold of Phil Townsend and pulled him in. Judge Quinton took a minute to enjoy the moment before concluding.

"Mr. John Stevens, I am happy to declare you're a free man and I extend the sincere apologies of this court. My only hope is that you have not lost your love for the law and that this ordeal will help you to be the best lawyer you can be. As for you Mr. Thomas Stevens, the confidence that you have exhibited in your son, the courage that you have shown in fighting for his release, and the tremendous service that you have performed for this city and the country will stand as an example for all of us. Good luck to both of you."

MAY ×× 2005